Tryouts

There were five more after me, but I didn't wait to see. . . . I went straight into the locker room, pulled my sweat pants right over my shorts, stuffed my other things into my gym bag, and went out. I was shaking all over.

At least they didn't post numerical scores. They weren't that cruel. They would announce the name of the winner, and nobody would know who came in second and who came in tenth.

Except me.

I'd know.

**Other Apple Paperbacks
you will enjoy:**

Aliens in the Family
  by Margaret Mahy

Almost Like a Sister
  by M.L. Kennedy

B, My Name Is Bunny
  by Norma Fox Mazer

Jeanne Up and Down
  by Jane Claypool Miner

Thirteen
  by Candice F. Ransom

THE RAH RAH GIRL

Caroline B. Cooney

AN
APPLE
PAPERBACK

SCHOLASTIC INC.
New York Toronto London Auckland Sydney

ISBN 0-590-33179-5

12 11 10 9 8 7 6 5 4 3 2 1   7 8 9/8 0 1 2/9

Printed in the U.S.A.   01

First Scholastic printing, June 1987

Chapter 1

My best friend Cath and I were watching *General Hospital* at my house. Cath can watch TV any time she wants, but my parents have firm anti-TV rules. One of these is that afternoon television is bad for you.

"You're the only person I know who sees a soap opera quarterly," said Cath. "This is your autumn sighting of the afternoon screen."

"When I have kids," I told her, "I will let them glue themselves to the tube."

"No, you won't, Marcy. You're a Kirk. Kirks don't come home from school and slouch around. You'll be just like your parents. You'll make your kids go out and achieve."

"Ugh," I said.

We took all the pillows off the couch and lined them up like toppled dominoes on the floor. Then we arranged ourselves over the pillows so that we could take turns braiding each other's hair. We just started growing our hair long a year and a half ago, and we are new to braiding. It's surprising how many ways you can arrange your hair around your skull once you learn. Cath has thin, straight dark hair that braids like silken strands. My hair is thick and very red. Sometimes I curl it till it sticks out around me like frizzled fire, and sometimes I smooth it down flat like carrot icing.

"I'm going to do one side in six little braids," Cath told me, "and then tease the rest. Maybe a talent scout will find you and let you cut a punk record."

But *General Hospital* came on, and we skipped braiding hair in favor of trying to figure out who this lean, dark, sulking young man was that neither of us recognized.

"I knew I shouldn't have gone to camp all summer," Cath wailed. "I don't even know this guy. It's obvious that everybody hates him. Do you think he's a conniving fiancé or a disinherited son blackmailing somebody?"

Naturally, an advertisement came on just as the dialogue was beginning to reveal clues.

"Ideally," said Cath, "we should have a bowl of potato chips in here. With sour cream-and-chive dip."

This would be possible at her house, but food is not allowed in the Kirk living room. My mother, who is in politics, entertains in here, and if the president of the chamber of commerce or the chairman of the finance committee sat down on the couch and crunched on old stale potato chips, Mom would strangle me. "We can pretend," I told Cath.

"I am too old to enjoy invisible potato chips," she said.

At this moment my mother came into the room. It was unexpected because she's usually in the office or at a meeting. "Hi, Mom," I said. "It's been ages since I've seen you in the afternoon."

"Hello, girls," she said, and she frowned.

The pillows, I thought. I'd never have tossed them on the floor if I'd known Mom was around. Not only were they lovely pillows (years ago my mother went through a pillow stage — before politics, of course — and made needlepoint, ribbon, quilted, and cross-stitch pillows), but the living room itself is very lovely. It's the only room in our house that *is*, because with both parents working full-time, and my sister and brother with both school and jobs, nobody even considers keeping more than one room presentable.

But my mother sat down on the dispillowed couch and did not appear to notice the difference. "Don't you have anything better to do than watch a soap opera, Marcy?" she asked.

Oh, that was the source of the frown. And it was a very tricky question, especially with a mother like mine. You see, my family does not believe in allowing time to lie around unused. Every single minute should count. In these minutes, you must be doing something meaningful, challenging, and rewarding. If it is for the greater good of humanity, all the better.

So if I said, "No, I don't have anything better to do than watch *General Hospital*," Mom would definitely find me something better to do. This might be scrubbing the bathroom, or it might be learning Arabic so I could become a world-famous diplomat later on in life.

And if I said, "Yes, I do have something better to do," then I would be expected to get right up and do it. And then I would never find out who the lean, dark, sulking young man was, or why everybody hated him.

And if I really took chances and said flippantly, "Mom, there *is* nothing better for a girl to do than watch *General Hospital*," I was in for a long and difficult discussion on the sort of values a ninth-grader ought to have acquired by now.

So I said brightly, "You know what happened in math today, Mom?"

Actually, very little had happened in math, so I had to improvise. I might have gotten away with it, too, except that Cath began to giggle into her pillows. "Really, Flame Brain," Cath said. "Can't you come up with a better story than that?"

My mother laughed in spite of herself. She is always a bit surprised by me, because I'm so unlike my brother and sister, but she usually stops short of open disapproval. And then, too, she likes the nickname Flame Brain. Only the "flame" part of the nickname is applicable, but Mom doesn't perceive it that way.

I think Flame Brain is dumb, but it certainly is preferable to some of the nicknames people end up with. Like George, who's called Twinkie because he eats so many of them. Or Roxanne, who once in first grade hurled mud at a kid who was bothering her and ever since then has been called Mudpie.

My mother is not easily deflected from a topic. Just because I had detoured into math and Cath had roadblocked with Flame Brain was no reason to stop her inquiry. "Surely you two have homework to do," she said.

"Nope." Cath answered for us. "First

week of school, Mrs. Kirk. Since we're ninth-graders and the big, big high school is scary and overwhelming, they're saving homework till next week."

"And is it," my mother asked, "scary and overwhelming?"

Cath and I giggled. "Considering we had orientation last spring," I said, "and a whole day of orientation before school started this week, it was an anticlimax. If anything, it's boring."

Being bored is a sin in my family. It's something you bring on yourself by being lazy and unimaginative.

After a few moments of fretting over this descent into boredom, Mom relaxed. "Oh, well. I suppose I mustn't worry. Your activities start up next week, and then you won't be frittering away valuable hours like this."

Cath sank into the pillow mound, drowning in embroidery. Once my activities started, we had to schedule our friendship. Nine minutes here, half a phone call there, alternate Sunday evenings there.

My activities.

I could see them . . . lined up like kids at a relay race.

I swallowed. I took a deep breath.

My mother is the mayor of our small city. You don't tangle with her over just anything. She whips governors who think our town is perfect for a new solid waste dump. She defeats belligerent unions and coaxes uncooperative managements into friendly agreements.

Cath peeped over a blue velvet pillow and nodded encouragingly. *Go ahead.* I chewed the brushy tip of a limp red braid that Cath had finished on the left side of my head. "Actually, Mom," I said, "I'm not sure I want to do all the things I did last year."

"Oh?" my mother said.

I have always felt I go to two schools at once. School school and after school. Anybody can muddle through school school, especially if she has a best friend like Cath and if English comes easily. But after school is something else again. Swim practice, soccer team, piano lessons, and Sunday school. Girl Scouts, outdoor education, Fair Isle knitting class, and ballet dancing.

Tuesdays, I thought dreamily. I believe it's Tuesdays I want free. A whole row of them. A white and empty parade of days on my calendar.

My mother does not respond to complaints. If you even think about whining, you may as well give up all hope. The city council learned early on that if they want my mother on their side, they'd better not moan and groan. The motto my mother lives by is, "Do it with a smile."

Dad and Claire and Tuck (my sister and

brother) find this easy. They'll have some horrible job to do, that would make anybody sick or furious or both, and they smile and do it pleasantly. I'm the only one who ever mutters and carries on. Once I even whined. The rest of the family couldn't believe I was related to them. Here I was with this red hair, that nobody else had ever had, and now I was whining. Probably somebody had switched babies at the hospital.

So it was in a gracious and calm voice that I said, "Mom, I believe I'd like to drop dancing class."

Cath and I had discussed this thoroughly. We came up with three possible answers:

1. Nonsense, Marcy. Dancing gives you poise.
2. Nonsense, Marcy. Dancing helps your coordination.
3. Nonsense, Marcy. We have a major investment in those lessons.

It was my theory that dancing lessons would go on the rest of my life whether I wanted them or not. It was Cath's theory that ninth grade was the year for freedom of choice, and if I didn't want dancing any more, I could quit.

I had told her, Well, maybe in *your* family it's called freedom of choice. In *my* family it's called marching orders. As for quitting, that is not a Kirk vocabulary word. Quitting shows a disgraceful lack of commitment and team spirit.

My mother watched an entire five minutes of *General Hospital* before she answered me. You could tell she could not believe we were actually sitting there paying attention to this drivel. Finally, she said, "Marcy, dear." I braced myself. "Marcy, I wouldn't force you into anything. Ever."

If Cath and I had not already been on the floor, we would have fallen there. My parents have a history of forcing me into *everything. Always.*

"If you want to drop dancing, you may," my mother said, and she smiled at me. "After all," she added, "you're in ninth grade now."

My jaw fell into the pillow beneath it, which happened to be a Flying Geese quilt pattern my mother stitched when she was pregnant with me. Ninth grade *is* the grade for freedom, I thought giddily.

Cath reached out with one long, thin index finger decorated on the tip with a long, thin, scarlet fingernail, and pushed my jaw back up where it belonged. We both giggled.

"Perhaps," my mother said meditatively, "you could call the community center."

"The community center?" I asked blankly. "No, Mom. I took from Anitra's School of Dance, remember?" How could she have forgotten all those humiliating dance recitals where I was always in the back row because I was always the one who forgot the steps? "I'll call them and let them know," I promised.

"To see what the community center is offering this year," she explained. "Let's see. Tuesday is your dance day. I'm sure they have something interesting on Tuesdays, Marcy. Maybe karate. Or needlepoint."

Cath burst into laughter. "Oh, Mrs. Kirk," she said, gasping and floundering on pillows as she laughed, "only you could mention karate and needlepoint in the same breath. And with a straight face, too."

"Catherine," said my mother, without a touch of humor, "I think this is a fine opportunity for Marcy to branch out into something else. Something unusual. Something that could be a new focus for her entrée into high school."

I stifled a moan and found a dark quiet spot under three pillows. Cath gave me a few moments by arguing with my mother. I love my parents very much, and they certainly love me, but it does not help our relationship at all that their first two children were Claire and Tuck.

My sister Claire studies hard. I don't even study often, let alone hard. Claire is always the head of a committee, whereas I don't even join them. Claire has hobbies that require strength of mind and body. She doesn't just stroll around the block, she trains for a marathon.

And Tuck. Of course, my brother Tuck is a jock. My mother and father did not have this in mind when they produced Tuck. They figured their son would be intelligent, sensitive, and willing to be a househusband, with a subspecialty in laundry. Well, he is all of those things — but he's also a jock.

Varsity, of course.

Both Tuck and Claire hold down part-time jobs. Tuck works at the grocery. He's a bag boy, and he always remembers to put the egg carton on top. If Tuck is going to do anything, he's going to do it well. It would not surprise any of us if they begged him to manage the entire grocery chain before he's eighteen.

Claire, my beautiful blonde sister Claire, pumps gas. She's out there all day Saturday and Sunday, in all kinds of terrible weather, washing windshields and checking oil.

My parents love it. A blow for women, a contribution to college funds, a step toward independence. All that.

Naturally, this is all an example for me to follow.

I often wish that I, Marcy, could have been born first. I'd have set examples for peace, quiet, daydreaming, and solitary pleasures. I came third, though, and these habits are referred to by the first Kirks as laziness, lack of team spirit, and slothfulness.

At least I can hang onto Tuesdays, I thought from under the pillow. So about calling the community center, I said, "Well, perhaps."

Because in my family when you make a commitment, it's for life. If I indicated the slightest interest in karate, or needlepoint, my mother would start me in a class, which would progress to private lessons. She'd buy handbooks and supplies and want to know when I was expecting my first award for excellence in my chosen field.

I emerged from the anonymity of my pillows to find my mother looking down at me, her chin cupped in her hands. She has an interesting face. It photographs well. She always looks very New England and stalwart, and people vote for her character as well as her record. Now there was a definite gleam in her eyes. She certainly wasn't gleaming over *General Hospital*, because she was talking right through it, putting quite a demand on Cath, who was determined to follow both dialogues, ours and the screen's. "Then what *are* you going to do?" asked Mother.

"Do?" I repeated.

"You know, Marcy," Cath said. With her hair braided tight, almost to the vanishing point, she looked pixie-ish and totally untrustworthy. "Are you going to take up scuba diving or become a collector of Alpine flowers? Are you going to learn COBOL or sell vacuum cleaners door to door?"

"Catherine, this is not a joke," my mother said, who nevertheless was laughing because she always laughs when it's Cath saying something. "Just because you are allowing all your considerable talents to go to waste is no reason to infect Marcy with the same nongoals."

Cath wasn't hurt. She and my mother have a running argument over whether Cath's talents are going to waste, or whether Cath just doesn't have any talent. It's a mystery to me that Cath and Mother remain on good terms, when all Mom ever does is lecture Cath on her poor use of valuable time.

"Mom, I don't think you understand," I said. "I don't want to add another activity. I want to drop one, and then I want to enjoy the free time."

"Free time?" my mother said.

"Like freedom of speech," said Cath helpfully. "Your daughter Marcy, here, is seeking freedom of time."

My mother laughed. "Well, of course everybody needs a little time to think," she agreed. It was an amazing statement, until I realized that while my definition of "a little time" was an afternoon, hers was "three minutes."

Mother glanced at the TV again, shook her head irritably, and studied a pillow she had stitched a decade earlier. Her tiny gold drop earrings leaped under the fringe of her short dark hair. Mother never changes her earrings because this consumes time, and she keeps her hair cut short so she can fix it briskly and easily when under pressure.

You'll never see me with a haircut like that. I love fooling with my hair.

Mother bent over me, kissed the top of my red head and ran her fingers through the half that wasn't braided yet. "I can't say I think it's wise to do nothing," she said, "but it's your decision, Marcy." From her jacket pocket (September through April my mother wears exclusively gray, navy, or scarlet wool suits) she pulled a list. She never moves without lists. She always has at least twelve imperative chores to be completed before dinner. Preferably before breakfast. There would never be an item that said, "Time out" or "Well-earned rest." I think Mom and Dad and Claire and Tuck rest by doing. I've watched them for fourteen years now and I've never seen one of them look forward to a moment of peace. It's not peaceful to them. It's irritating.

In a moment she got up, all this leisure time getting on her nerves, and went to the kitchen telephone, so she could both discuss an urgent matter and have a cup of coffee. Always do two things at once.

"See?" said Cath triumphantly, punching me through the pillows. "What did I tell you? Ninth grade is the grade for freedom."

I envisioned that row of Tuesdays. All mine. Empty.

We turned the television off and went for a long walk. The leaves had not yet turned, and the September air was still warm. We bought slushies at the corner store. There were two eleventh-grade boys there getting Cokes from the vending machine. They stood and talked to us for a while. *Us.* Ninth-grade girls. They knew our names, our teachers, and our swim team! When they left, Cath and I stared after them.

"Those are Tuck's friends," I marveled. "I never thought the day would come when a friend of Tuck's would associate with me."

"They liked us," Cath said. She repeated the words very softly to herself, like a prize or a secret. *"They liked us."*

I'll spend my free Tuesdays like this, I thought. A best friend, a walk, a slushie, some boys.

Beats dancing class any time.

We walked home silently.

Cath picked the first fallen scarlet leaf from the sidewalk and traced its jagged edges in her palm. I stared up at the deep blue sky, free of clouds, free of wind, waiting for change, and I thought . . . but I could drop *all of it*! Not just dancing, but all the other things jammed into my life just because Claire and Tuck jammed them into their lives.

I could make my own choices. I could choose to do nothing, or I could take karate or needlepoint.

This year it would be *my* time.

To divide and use as *I* chose.

It was an idea as dizzy and glorious as the blue autumn sky, as piercing as the angled rays of the setting sun.

Chapter 2

Although I don't think of myself as a typical Kirk, once I make up my mind to accomplish something, I do it in record time. By the third week of September, I had extricated myself from every single after school activity I had ever been in.

Now you would think, in a family where character and style are everything, that when a person strikes out on her own, going down new paths and taking untrodden roads, she would get a little support.

You would expect her father to say, "Oh, Marcy, I'm so proud of you, going your way, setting your own standards."

You would expect her mother to cry, "Oh, Marcy, clearly we've done well with you, just look at how you can disregard the common run of activity."

Well, you would be wrong.

My parents were appalled.

Their attitude was that I was destroying myself.

I quit soccer, explaining I'd rather watch than play. I quit outdoor ed., because although I like canoeing, hiking, and hawkwatching. I have done enough of that, and it wasn't even my idea to start with. I quit Spanish Club because five periods a week of Spanish is quite enough, even if they do bribe you with free Cokes.

Now Tuck and Claire were *using* their abilities. But I — I had had potential once, and in three short weeks I threw it all away, with a total disregard for the years of effort I had invested.

"Marcy," said my mother, truly horrified. "It isn't that I deeply believe in any one of those activities. It's that it's so unhealthy to be inactive. You have to *do* something."

"I will," I promised. I will see more of *General Hospital*, I thought. I will take more walks, meet more boys, have another slushie.

"You're going to be bored if you don't do something," my father said anxiously. My father got bored with a corporate job, left to start not one but *two* small businesses of his own in order to stave off boredom.

"Don't worry, Dad," I told him. "I'm just clearing the horizon."

They were pacified. Marcy was going to spend a brisk, efficient weekend clearing her horizons, and then she'd erupt like a typical Kirk whirlwind with a whole new assortment of activities.

Cath, of course, saw through my excuses. She knew perfectly well that once I got my horizons clear, I'd leave them that way. "By Monday," she warned, "they're going to suspect that in your case the horizons are activity free."

I pointed to a pile of library books. All of them had titles like *Your Career in Social Work, Your Career in Computer Technology, Your Career in the Coast Guard.* "I'll keep checking this kind of book out," I told Cath. "A smokescreen. They'll think I'm concentrating on my future when all I'm really doing is lugging heavy books around."

"Flame Brain, you are very shifty," Cath said. "If I had known you had this sneaky streak in you, I'm not sure I would have become such intimate friends."

I snorted. "You're intimate friends with me because you're exactly my type."

"Oh, Marcy, don't even say such a thing. I am lazy. I am utterly lacking in goals, and my inner drive registers zero. You, on the other hand, are a Kirk. Kirks are energetic, highly motivated achievers."

"So my parents tell me. Do you realize,

Cath, that at this moment in life I have not got a single commitment except two pages of algebra? I don't have anything to practice, hone, change, work on, or learn."

"Are you bored?" Cath asked.

"No."

"You're going to get bored."

"Never."

And I wasn't. I loved the free time. Little things came up, unmemorable things I enjoyed at the time, and the days passed in peaceful, satisfying, undemanding sequence.

With the exception, of course, of those minutes when my mother nagged me to join something, or my father wanted to know where my team spirit was.

They actually took me to the doctor to see if I had mononucleosis, because nothing less than disease could keep a Kirk down like this.

The whole atmosphere at home became suspicious. Kirks didn't hang around. Yet there, right in the same room, indubitably, was a Kirk hanging around.

My mother began clipping little articles from the newspaper about successful women. I'd find them pinned to my bedspread, or sitting at my breakfast place, or resting on top of my piled school books. I am not kidding when I say that she actually packed a lunch for me (unheard of to begin with; I've been packing my own since third grade) and stuck an article in with my chocolate mint cookies.

My father was equally tense. "Want to go for a walk with me, Marcy?"

"Sure." I love going anywhere with my father.

Half a mile from home, he'd spoiled the walk by asking if there was anything serious I wanted to confess to him.

The first few times, I sighed and reassured him that I really was fine, perfectly fine. Then it began to irk me. What did they think I was *doing*?

It was known throughout the entire high school that war had been declared in the Kirk household. My friends thought it was a wonderful joke. They were always asking what my mother had suggested for me to do this week.

"Are you scheduled to become the East Coast winter grass-cutting champion?" somebody would ask.

"She's too busy," another kid would retort. "She's training to become the barbed wire collector of the decade."

It was a slow fall for gossip.

My situation became the ninth grade's favorite topic.

Will Marcy shave her head and put a safety pin through her nose, or will she submit to her parents' demands and surpass Claire and Tuck combined?

And of course I knew that if I did take something up — photography say, since I have always yearned to be a camerawoman on television — why, my mother would fling herself into it with such joy that she'd have me interning on the local paper, entering photographic contests, taking night classes, doing comparative shopping for the best movie cameras, and building my own developing lab, when all I really wanted was to snap a few pictures now and then.

Cath and I spent a lot of time lying around on the floor pillows discussing ourselves. We were the two most interesting subjects we knew. Best friends are so decent. Best friends never tell you to chair the activities program or star in the drama production. Best friends tell you you're perfect just the way you are and that any day now someone equally perfect is going to notice and ask you out. When you tell a best friend all that matters is getting rid of a pimple on your chin, she doesn't say you should be worrying about American foreign policy instead.

"Do you think I'm ordinary?" I asked Cath.

"I think you're extraordinary," she said. "You have such guts, standing up to four Kirks at a time, week in and week out."

I contemplated the vision of myself as a tough, gutsy woman. Very satisfying. "Do you think I'm nice-looking, though?"

"Very."

"I'm pear shaped," I said. "My figure is in reverse."

"No, it isn't. Especially in cold weather, when heavy pullover sweaters cover a multitude of problems."

"Just half of them."

"Wasn't last week's football game wonderful, cheering for Tuck?" Cath said dreamily.

"He's good," I agreed. I went to games half to see my brother play and half to enjoy the cheerleading. I'm not that fond of sports but I love cheerleading. Of course, my mother thinks it's the pits, and Claire considers all cheerleaders to be empty-headed rah-rahs. A Woman For Our Time would never be a cheerleader. "All my family does these days is wait for my niche to appear," I told Cath.

"It will," she said comfortingly. "Meanwhile, it's a good thing you're a Kirk. Otherwise you wouldn't have the strength for all this fighting."

"Fighting? I'm not fighting. I'm lying around doing nothing."

"You're rebelling," Cath said. "Your parents didn't go through any rebellion with Claire and Tuck, who are perfect, and you're determined to rebel enough for all three."

"I could argue with your statement that Claire and Tuck are perfect."

"No," my mother said loudly from the next room, where she was working on reports from the Sewer Commission. "Marcy is not rebelling. She's just lazy."

So now it was out in the open, where we could kick it around. Four Kirks were hardworking, industrious, interesting people. One Kirk was just plain lazy.

Sometimes I seriously considered going to live with a loving aunt or uncle. Only the fact that neither my father nor my mother ever had any brothers and sisters stopped me.

"Do anything today?" Claire said one night at dinner, her voice implying that if I had done anything, she would faint from the shock. Claire, of course, had gotten a ninety in all the day's quizzes; she had worked out at the Y to stay in shape, pumped gas for two hours, telephoned her committee members about the fundraiser for the AFS, and there she was, her long blonde hair perfectly neat on her gray chamois shirt.

I had made dinner and set the table. Being the only nonbusy person in the family had also made me responsible for evening meals, the quality of which was deteriorating every night. I had learned that cooking is very boring. Cleanup is even boringer.

Supper consisted of microwaved frozen chicken pot pies dumped out over Minute Rice with spoonfuls of canned peas and biscuits that I wrenched free from a refrigerator can.

To compensate for the lack of gourmet food, I had set the table with cloth napkins, silver, and bayberry candles. The room was scented with a combination of bayberry, chicken, Claire's perfume, and Tuck's sweat.

"A big day for you," Claire observed, ignoring the fact that I had not only done dinner but even lit two candles, "is a video game and a low score."

"Now, girls," my father said. He wants peace in the world and feels it should begin at the dinner table.

Tuck was struggling to butter a roll. I had forgotten to take the butter out of the freezer to soften, so this meant chipping little hunks of butter off and decorating the roll like a cookie with M&M's.

Suddenly, my brother Tuck, my own flesh and blood, said, "Do you think Marcy has a psychological problem?"

Now Tuck never says anything unkind about me, mostly because he never says anything about me at all. He's much too sophisticated to care about some dumb ninth-grader who happens to be related to him.

"*Many* psychological problems," said Claire. We have shared a room all our lives, and if I *do* have any psychological problems, then Claire has given them to me.

"I'm serious," Tuck said. "I think there's something wrong with her. She just hangs around. It's spooky."

"I don't know that it's spooky," my father said, "but I agree that she has become rather low-key these days."

"I think she's mentally sick," Claire said. "That's what you can do to fill up her time, Mother. Send her to a shrink."

"Claire, you are not being helpful," my mother said. "Marcy is not sick. She's just—"

"*Here*!" I yelled. "I am right here, sitting at the very same table. Don't talk about me as if I'm in Peru."

"If only you were," Claire said. I thought of all the nights I turned off my bed light early just because she gets tired before I do, and I regretted every single time.

"Sometimes you might as well be in Peru, Marcy," my mother said. "I think we're all agreed that you can't be a spectator all your life. You have to get out there and achieve."

It was my moment to lean forward and say, "But I *am* going to be a spectator all my life. I'm going to be the most careful, artistic, thoughtful spectator the world has ever seen. I'm going to be sought after by ABC, NBC, and CBS. I'm going to spectate at the world's most exciting moments. The pivots in history. I am going to. You just wait!"

But Tuck was tired of the subject of Marcy. Claire was spooning more canned peas onto her plate, even though she feels they are a sickly green and not the same as real peas, and she, Claire, ought to have fresh broccoli with lemon sauce.

So I didn't tell them a thing.

I said, "I do not have a psychological problem, Tuckerman Kirk. I am doing exactly what I want to be doing."

"Which is not a whole lot," Claire said.

Sisters!

"Stop this! I *do* have interests. I'm regrouping," I said with dignity. "I'm reassessing my position and pretty soon, I'm going to emerge."

"You studied your vocabulary list anyhow," Claire said.

"Careful, Claire," Tuck said. "Marcy may emerge as a murderer, and you'll be the victim."

"What a good idea," I said.

My father said that if he heard any more of this, he would abandon all of us.

My mother said that dealing with striking hospital workers was infinitely more pleasant than being home with her own children.

Tuck said he had a lot of important homework to do.

Claire said she had important phone calls to make. (Would a girl of Claire's stature ever have boring, unimportant phone calls to make?)

My father said, "Then you can do the dishes, please, Marcy, since you have nothing else to do."

I scraped those dishes with rage in my heart. I slam-stacked that dishwasher. When I ran the garbage disposal in the sink, I heard the sounds of my perfect siblings' bones crunching.

Revenge, I thought. I'll make them pay. They want to mold me as if I'm made of modeling clay. Well, when I emerge, it will be as Marcy Kirk herself, not as whatever creature half mixed from Tuck and Claire they have in mind.

I tried to think of a way to give them as hard a time as they were giving me.

But nothing came to mind.

Chapter 3

One thing for sure, neither my parents nor I intended me to fill any of this free time by getting detention.

After all, it was Friday, and I like Fridays. Fridays are short and cozy and you can just feel the weekend waiting for you. On Fridays all problems are surmountable and all weather acceptable. Friday night seems long and thick, with lots of room for staying up late and no setting an alarm clock for a chilly dawn.

Cath would be sleeping over, and on Saturday we were going to a football game. The day was supposed to be clear and sunny and reasonably mild. All through school I felt clear and sunny and reasonably mild.

Unfortunately, we had a substitute in music history.

Nobody in the ninth grade asked for music history. We didn't ask for art history, either, but the school is experimenting on us and we have two hours a week of each. Everybody admits that ninth grade is a particularly difficult year in which to instill anything in anyone, let alone culture, but nevertheless, on Fridays, we listen to Great Music and get a lecture on its composer and its place in history.

Dr. Payne teaches it. He's a retired college professor, short and gentle with a voice so soft you have to stop breathing to hear it. Dr. Payne can make the tragic life of Mozart or the frustrating existence of Bach seem more important than anything else in school.

But Dr. Payne was ill.

Substitutes never teach anyway, but they're infinitely worse not teaching music history than they are not teaching math. In music there is nothing to do but sit on a chair, with not even a desk to rest your elbows on, waiting for the period to end.

The sub was Mr. Oones. Mr. Oones is your basic primate. He breathes and stands erect and has the use of an opposing thumb. There's a possibility that careful training could teach him to retrieve.

Twenty-seven of us walked into the room, stopped short, and groaned, "Mr. Oones."

Mr. Oones beamed happily at the way we always remembered his name. "Now, children," he began. This was not auspicious.

We don't like being addressed that way. "I was not left a lesson plan," said Mr. Oones fussily, implying that Dr. Payne was seriously remiss in not leaving one. We love Dr. Payne and we didn't like the criticism. "What we're going to do is listen to tapes of the Brandenburg Concertos."

Nobody objected to that.

"You may even study at the same time!" Mr. Oones added, as if this were a splendid treat.

"Oh, wow, thanks," Twinkie said. "Can we *really?* Golly, Mr. Oones."

Mr. Oones retired behind the desk to read a paperback. The orange sticker on the book meant he'd bought the paperback second-hand, and as the pages fell to the floor every time he turned one, it may well have been nineteenth hand. We argued over whether Mr. Oones was capable of noticing the missing pages as he read.

Very slowly, over a ten-minute time span, Twinkie turned up the volume on the tape player until the whole room was quivering with Bach. Mr. Oones noticed nothing. His pages continued to flutter to the floor like maxi-confetti.

"I have something to tell you," Cath said in an undertone. By now the Brandenburgs were so loud that an undertone was practically a shout.

We climbed up on the concert bleachers,

which are stored in the back of the room and not intended for actual use except when they're carted out to the stage. Mr. Oones didn't see us going. It was hot up there, close to the lights, and I felt so sleepy I stretched out on a riser.

"What are you doing up there, Flame Brain?" Twinkie yelled. The Brandenburgs were now so loud the chalk was dancing on the blackboard rim. "Getting a tan?"

"Right," I said.

Mudpie said that she could not figure out how I expected to get a tan with six layers of clothing on.

We laughed and Cath said, "It *is* ridiculous to be so burdened down by fabric." Cath took off her jacket (our school is boiling in some rooms and frigid in others, so intelligent people travel well equipped to strip or add) and then peeled off her wool plaid vest.

The boys began making wisecracks. I have to admit some of these were a little crude.

I, being thrilled by the Friday atmosphere and the deafening pulse of Bach, began by unlacing my boots. I was wearing high chestnut-brown leather boots, soft and squashy with leather thongs.

Cath toyed with the top button of her oxford shirt. Under this shirt she was wearing a thick yellow turtleneck pullover, so even if she were to undo every single button on the shirt, she'd still be covered from her chin down.

I checked to see if David Summer was fully appreciating me, displayed there on the top riser with my left boot untied, but of course he was the only one in the room who had not noticed that anything was happening.

I forgot about Mr. Oones.

I was just about to untie my other boot lace when Mrs. Arrington, our principal, turned off the tape player with a flick of the wrist that practically broke the fragile knob, and screamed at Cath and me to get down off there and stop disrupting the class.

I had forgotten that Mr. Oones knew his limitations, and had been known to call for reinforcements.

Once the music stopped, we were just two silly girls with untied shoes, stranded on the upmost concert riser. Absolutely nothing had happened, yet we were about to get into trouble. It's like breaking your leg falling out of your own bed. Embarrassing. You ought to break bones on the ski slopes and have a little class. And if you're going to get into trouble in music history, it ought to be something with more substance than untying your boots.

"Marcy Kirk!" said Mrs. Arrington. "I

am simply shocked. A girl with your background."

"She didn't do anything," Cath said. "Really, Mrs. Arrington, nothing happened. We're both very sorry." She turned to Mr. Oones. "I'm really sorry, Mr. Oones. One thing just led to another."

"Well!" said Mrs. Arrington grimly. "It's good I got here before you entered the final stage."

"No, no," we protested weakly. "There wasn't going to be another stage. We were just being silly. We — "

Mrs. Arrington swept us out of the music room and down to her office. Neither Cath nor I had ever been in trouble before, and neither of us wanted to be now. We pointed out that we weren't vandalizing the school or even being rude to Mr. Oones. We certainly had not done *anything*.

"It's the thought that counts," Mrs. Arrington said.

"We weren't thinking of *doing* anything," we protested.

"The *boys* were thinking it," said Mrs. Arrington. "Six hours. Who ever would have thought that the sister of Claire and Tuck would behave in such a manner?"

I thought she meant that for six hours I had behaved in a manner that did not reflect well on Claire and Tuck. "No, really,

Mrs. Arrington," I said, "it was only for a few minutes. We — "

"Six hours of detention," she said, "and no lip."

Six hours.

We were in ninth grade now.

It went on permanent records.

Cath and I exchanged horrified looks. We didn't give Mrs. Arrington any lip, although we certainly entertained some evil thoughts about her. All through the rest of school I thought, *six hours*. My parents will throw me to the lions.

I made a fatal decision.

I would not tell my parents about the detention until Sunday night. Otherwise the whole weekend would be ruined. And aside from Cath coming over and the football game, my parents were in a wonderfully giddy mood, having made a very important pair of decisions themselves.

Mother had definitely decided to run the following fall for state senate. Dad had decided to sell one of his two businesses in order to have time to help in the campaign, and generally be home a lot more when she won, because she would be up at the state capital for weeks at a time.

Into this atmosphere was I going to toss my detention?

Into this success and joy was I going to say that Marcy had exchanged her policy of doing nothing for a policy of serious misbehavior?

I'll wait until Sunday night, I thought. Maybe by then I'll have thought of a good way to describe the whole thing.

The cheerleaders were wearing thick sweaters with the school letter. Their pompons rustled like leaves being raked. My brother Tuck had just scored a goal, we were winning, and the stands were shuddering from the thumping feet of happy fans.

Cath and I were wrapped in a thick plaid blanket. She had most of the blanket and I had most of the fringe, but I wasn't arguing because I was in my new ski jacket, thick and silken like a parachute, in a soft dark green that set off my hair perfectly. I always felt wonderful in that jacket. My favorite class was algebra, because it was so cold on the north side of the building we had to wear our coats.

"Oh, no," Cath said. "Oh, Marcy, look who just sat down next to your mother and father."

Mrs. Arrington.

It didn't take a genius to know what they were going to talk about. I should have thought of this, I told myself. I should have remembered that Mrs. Arrington comes to all the games, and my parents come to all the games, and the mayor always chats with the high school principal.

Mrs. Arrington's hair was graying. She parted it in the middle and fixed it in a little knot. I could see her bald spot perfectly in spite of the knot. My father was wearing a gray tweed cap that sat jauntily on his smooth dark hair. He looked like someone about to speed off for a road rally in his Porsche. My mother had tied a square of fringed navy wool over her hair, and she looked young and carefree. From up here she and my father looked like high school students conferring with their elderly principal over the college applications.

But they weren't.

They were talking about Marcy and how bad she was.

"Sway to the left!" shrieked the cheerleaders, starting a spirit cheer. "Sway to the right! Stand up! Sit down! Fight, fight, FIGHT!"

Cath and I swayed, stood up, sat down, and yelled. Mrs. Arrington stayed right where she was. My parents stood up, but only to see over the cheerleaders' heads so they could watch Tuck without interference.

If only I'd told Mom and Dad on Friday! I wish my brain had an early warning system, so little bells would go off when I'm making particularly stupid decisions.

The squad ended with a perfectly timed series of squat jumps and pompon circles: like a wave on the beach, with pompons for white caps. From here you couldn't tell their sweaters were so old they were having a car wash to raise money for new ones.

"I don't see why we had to get so much detention," Cath said. "I thought it was pretty funny."

"Substitutes never think anything is funny. They think their authority is being undermined."

"Dyna — MO
Let's GO!
Dyna — MITE
Let's FIGHT!"

We yelled with the cheerleaders. They finished with a formation of double thigh stands, until they were three girls high. Nancy Bloom couldn't seem to keep her balance and took three tries to get up. I died for her.

"Hey, Flame Brain!" yelled one of the boys on the bottom bleacher. "How many hours did you get?"

"Six!" I yelled, thinking, what a way to announce this to my parents.

"Way to go, Marcy!" he shouted in

rhythm, like a cheer. He and two other boys shook their fists triumphantly at this good news.

My father turned and inspected me for a long moment, as though making absolutely sure this really was his daughter. He moved one index finger in a commanding, beckoning way.

"This is called facing the music," I said to Cath. "It's all over for me now." I gave her the rest of the blanket.

"They have their images to think of," she pointed out. "They can't be out there abusing their daughter in public."

"They can't have a daughter getting detention, either."

"It's not as if you're going to make a habit of it," said Cath. "Now go down and take your lecture like the tough Kirk you are. And stay there for a while. I want the whole blanket."

"What a friend," I muttered. I picked my way between thermos bottles and feet until I landed in an empty spot just behind and above my parents. They were looking stern and uncompromising.

I hate being corrected.

I think that's one reason I was so willing to give up all my lessons. Here's what a lesson is: You do your best; your teacher tells you it isn't good enough.

I always get mad at them.

Like now, being mad at Mr. Oones and Mrs. Arrington and my parents as well, and not being angry at myself at all.

But before I could say anything to my mother and father, someone above me grabbed my hair and pulled my head backward. From upside down I recognized Hawk Pietro. He's a senior. They call him Hawk because he has a nose like one. Hawk is a baseball man with no sport to pursue during football season. "Hullo, Hawk," I said, trying to disentangle myself with the least possible pain.

"Hey, Flame Brain. How are ya?"

"Not too good. I got detention for hacking around in music."

"I heard. I have detention, too. I cut biology lab three times in a row. I'll see you there." Hawk gave my hair a final tug, leaped lightly off the bleachers and trotted away.

Boys are always going off on mysterious errands.

My mother's expression deserved to be immortalized in a Hall of Fame for Shocked Parents. "*Hawk*?" she said. She would like me to have crushes on people who are exchange students from Paris, or winners of the Westinghouse Science Competition.

"We're just friends, Mom," I said. "Mom, I'm sorry I didn't tell you about the detention. I didn't want to spoil your weekend."

My mother accepted this. Where her children are concerned, she has some blind spots. My father doesn't. He looked at me with twice the disappointment of before. "You mean you didn't want to spoil *your* weekend," he said.

I flushed and could not meet his eyes. He didn't add to his statement. He never does. I tried to think of reasons to defend a position I knew was wrong. "It's not a big thing," I said stiffly. "Nothing serious happened in music at all, and there was no reason in the world to give Cath and me detention over it."

"I have to disagree with you, Marcy," my mother said. "I think it's very serious."

"We're not happy watching you disintegrate," my father said.

"I'm not disintegrating," I said irritably. "The detention is just a fluke. I wasn't bad, I was just silly."

"Forget the detention," my mother said quietly.

I stared at her. She was willing to forget the detention? What is so wonderful as an understanding parent? "Oh, Mom," I said, hugging her. "Thank you so much. I knew you'd understand. I knew you'd — "

"No," she said. "I don't understand. I

don't understand any of this. What is happening to you, Marcy?"

"You don't have to become unglued over one dumb afternoon," I said. I wanted to leap up and down and scream, but I had to sit there talking quietly so just the three of us could hear.

"We're not unglued over one dumb afternoon," my father said. "We're unglued over an entire school year of dumb afternoons. You quit Spanish, dancing, outdoor ed., swimming ... everything you've ever done."

"I wanted some free time."

"You've got it," my father agreed. "The question is, what made you suddenly want this?"

How often do they expect me to explain? I thought furiously. How often do I have to go over the same ground?

My mother said, very carefully, very slowly, "Sometimes they say when a teenager removes herself from her usual spheres and becomes very different from what she was before that this is a sign of. . . ."

She didn't finish. She didn't look at me. She took one deep breath after another and folded her fingers through each other until the rings bit into her flesh. She hadn't been that nervous the day she went on television for a live debate in the mayoral race.

Understanding flooded me, and with it,

rage. "Oh, Mother!" I said, barely managing to keep my voice under control. "Honestly, don't you have any faith in me at all? I'm not taking drugs! I'm not drinking! Please stop worrying about me. I can't *stand* this."

I was really deeply offended. How *could* they?

It hurt more than I had ever thought such a thing could.

And on top of that insult, they'd discussed this fear with bald old Mrs. Arrington. Mrs. Arrington gossiped. She'd tell every teacher in school that our mayor had a problem child in the family, too.

"We've talked to several people about it," said my father. "Your former scout leader. Your former piano teacher. . . ."

It was quite a list. I had formerly associated with a lot of people.

"And they felt you just needed a change," my mother said. "That there was nothing seriously wrong."

The implication being that there was a whole lot wrong, but we were going to wait another week before admitting that it was serious.

Don't explode, I said to myself. You can see how they'd arrive at that possibility. You can go on living with them even though they call in nine paid consultants just because you want to lead your life your way.

"I'm also worrying about your relationship with Hawk," Mom said.

"Mom, Hawk is just a person in school. I don't have any association with him whatsoever."

"You will have in detention," she pointed out.

"Nobody associates with anybody in detention, Mother. You sit with an empty desk between everybody and you study."

"How do you know so much about detention?" she demanded.

I closed my eyes. "All this trust," I said to her. "It's overwhelming."

And she said to me, "So I was right in the beginning, wasn't I?"

"Were you?" I said, feeling acid remarks surfacing, and trying to neutralize them.

"You're just lazy," she said.

Chapter 4

The world changed on Saturday, the 22nd of November.

It was very gray and cold and threatening either nasty rain or light snow. Like all other close relatives and diehard fans, we were at a football game.

Tuck, of course, was on the team, scoring points, and being a hero.

And Claire, good old superlative Claire, was doing the radio coverage. She was at this very moment the first girl in our county to do live coverage of a high school football game.

My parents were bursting with pride. Each of them was wearing an earphone radio so they could hear Claire, and they were sitting in the middle of the bleachers for the best possible view of Tuck.

I sat directly behind them with Cath and Munson, a girl one year older than us, who, for some reason, is always called by her last name. We would not have sat that close to my parents, given the present hostile relationship, except that my mother was in possession of the food and drinks. We had demolished the potato chips, finished the roast beef sandwiches, and started in on the cold potato salad. We hadn't seen much of the game, but there was plenty to come, so we weren't worried.

Munson wanted to know who I had a crush on right now.

"The field is open," I told her. "I rather like a lot of boys, but I can't get excited about any of them."

"I know what you mean," Munson agreed. "They're not complete jerks, but they're not high-quality romance, either."

"Do you think the boys talk about us the way we talk about them?" Cath wanted to know.

"My brother certainly doesn't," I said.

Naturally, Munson and Cath crowded close to hear what my brother the football hero talked about.

"Nothing," I said. "Heros are always nonverbal."

My mother gave me an exasperated look.

"How did you hear me say that?" I asked her. "I thought you were listening to Claire?"

"A used car ad came on," she said. "I turned the volume down."

"Quick," said Munson, "somebody bring up a meaningful topic."

My mother laughed.

I guess I am basically a very forgiving homebody type. It's hard to be at war with somebody you like, and I like my mother. I like her laugh, and the way she always goes to everything, no matter how tired she is. Claire. Now, I could go on loathing Claire till I'm a grandmother. But whenever I see Mom in action, I soften.

"Oh, what a super cheer!" Cath cried. "Did you see that?

"Is there any more roast beef?" Munson asked.

"What cheer?" I said. "I didn't see a thing. No, there's only baloney left."

"Not our cheerleaders, their cheerleaders," Cath said. "I absolutely loved their footwork."

"Although I think you should have been more encouraging to Marty Iler," said Munson. "He has quite a bit to offer. I guess if there's only baloney, I'm not hungry."

"Their squad isn't as good as ours," I told Cath, "but they're very creative. It makes up for skill."

"Oh, Marcy!" my mother cried, establishing once and for all that she was not listening to Claire: She was listening to us.

47

"How can you sit there talking about boy-friends and cheerleading? Honestly! There must be a thousand more interesting topics."

Munson whispered, "Is she serious?"

"Very," Cath whispered back. "When you're a mayor, you're always serious."

"I detest cheerleaders," my mother said.

Our squad started a sideline cheer and shifted down several paces in our direction. The people behind them stood up to see the action, and that meant my parents had to stand up to see over *them*, and the stands rippled with action.

"What's wrong with cheerleading, Mrs. Kirk?" Munson asked.

"It's an affront to women. It's nothing but leaping around praising the boys, who are the ones out there actually doing the work and taking the risks. It's one of the more bizarre activities humankind has ever dreamed up. Elementary dance steps, screaming, uniforms designed to attract boys, and absolutely no purpose whatso-ever."

"Wow," said Munson, who had definitely not expected quite so thorough an answer. "Heavy."

But Munson is like Cath. She's never serious for long, if at all. "I love those uniforms though, Mrs. Kirk. I think all they are is short, and maroon and white, but if they also attract boys I'm going to try out for the squad."

"Did you know that Pammy Feingold is moving?" said Munson.

Our heads turned toward the field. Pammy was doing a cheer for Tuck, who had apparently accomplished something when I wasn't looking. "How awful for her," I said. "She just made the squad this year, and she's been trying since she was a freshman."

Munson nodded. "Yup. Her father got transferred to California."

"Oh, well, that makes up for it," I said. "Anybody would jump at the chance to go to California, even if it meant dropping out of the cheerleading squad."

Suddenly Cath sucked in her breath, as if she'd just gotten a paper cut, or a cramp. I looked at her, ready to offer help, but she was just fiddling with her sneaker laces. Cath is the only person I know who changes her laces the way other people change their underwear. She has shoelaces with hearts, unicorns, rainbows, teddy bears, sailboats, and ducks. "You realize, of course, what this means," said Cath very quietly. So my mother, with or without earphones, would not hear.

"What what means?" I murmured.

"Pammy Feingold moving away."

"No. What does it mean?"

"It means there's an opening on the squad," Cath said.

"So?"

"So I think you'd make a terrific cheerleader. Here you are with that glorious mane of red hair just aching to be displayed in front of the crowds. Here you are with years of athletic training and dancing class that need an outlet. Here you are with roughly nine times the potential of attracting boys as Munson."

"I resent that," said Munson.

I shook my head. "My parents would die before they let me cheerlead," I said.

"Precisely," said Cath.

We examined the squad. I pictured myself where Pammy Feingold was, three from the right. Pammy was hopping up and down with excitement, watching the action on the field.

"An interesting solution to a current dilemma," Cath said. "Think of all cheerleading has to offer. A high moral tone, for example. You can't participate if you drink, swear, smoke, use drugs, or act crudely. And it requires energy and effort. A six-day-a-week commitment."

"That's true," I said thoughtfully. "And it means team spirit, civic duty, and public appearances."

Cath and I began to giggle. We laughed until we fell against each other, knocked

Munson half off the bleacher, and spilled the last of the potato salad to the grass six feet below.

Cath tapped my mother on the shoulder.

This is it, I thought. Perfect revenge. And Claire would go berserk. She thinks only total morons even consider cheerleading. Now she'll have to watch her little sister out there every single game.

"Mrs. Kirk?" Cath said, looking her most pixie-ish and untrustworthy.

"Yes, Cath. Would you like hot apple cider or hot chocolate?"

"Hot chocolate, please," Cath said. While my mother was bent over pouring this from her thermos, Cath said to me, "Marcy, I can't hurt a woman who offers me both hot apple cider and hot chocolate."

We all accepted mugs of steaming liquid. It was too hot to swallow, and we just wrapped our fingers around the china and felt its warmth seeping into our flesh.

Munson said, as if we'd coached her, "Mrs. Kirk, I don't really grasp your view of cheerleaders. I mean, if, for example, just suppose that Marcy became a cheerleader. How would you feel about that?"

Both my parents nearly spilled their drinks.

"*My* daughter?" my mother said. "I would rather my daughter caught *lice* than become a cheerleader."

Chapter 5

Claire and Tuck can remember a time when Mother was not in politics. They say we used to eat in the dining room and have wonderful meals with homemade cranberry-nut muffins and a first course of some interesting thick soup, like pumpkin onion.

I happen to hate cranberries, nuts, pumpkins, and onions, and I'm glad that while Mother was making meals like that I was having peanut butter sandwiches with the crusts cut off.

Now we're on a regular cycle.

There's Claire's night. She orders pizza. Although once last year she heated up a jar of spaghetti sauce and cooked a box of spaghetti and slathered butter over French bread. We were overwhelmed.

There's Tuck's night. Tuck orders grinders. Sometimes he orders meatball grinders, and sometimes he orders sausage and pepper grinders.

My father actually cooks. His night is a roast, with potatoes lying in the juice, mashed squash, rolls, and spinach salad. I'm the one who has to wash the spinach. Dad says he doesn't notice the grit, and Claire and Tuck won't touch raw spinach, so they don't care if it's gritty or not.

My mother's nights don't come up very often. She's usually just home from one meeting and on her way to the next. If it's her turn, she stops at the deli for fried chicken and potato salad.

That night it was my turn. I felt adventuresome. I located a cookbook, dusted it off, and made a casserole of chicken, onion, parsley, garlic, and beer, with fat noodles and a last minute addition of frozen peas (so they're bright green, not hospital green like canned peas), and topped it with crushed potato chips, parmesan cheese, and flecks of mozzarella.

My family was stunned.

Real food. Cooked in *our* oven, with *our* ingredients. For the first time in Kirk history, there was no conversation. Now, we always converse. For one thing, dinner is the only time we're apt to be together. For another, my mother is always hot under the collar about some local problem, and my father is always ready to yell about some federal regulation that's interfering with his business.

That night, nobody talked. There were happy sounds: slurping, chewing sounds. Five contented Kirks chowed down. You could feel everybody wishing that either we could hire a housekeeper, or that Marcy would always be in a cooking mood, or that we lived next door to a restaurant that served this food daily at incredibly reasonable prices.

"I'm trying out for cheerleading," I said.

I helped myself to more noodles. Ordinarily I would be careful of overeating, but I figured with all the exercise I was going to get being a cheerleader, I could relax about calories.

My mother said, "I beg your pardon, Marcy?"

"I'm trying out for cheerleading. Pammy Feingold's moving. They did have an extra on the squad just in case somebody did drop off, but the extra was Janet Andersen, and she left in September for boarding school." I chewed noodles. "So there's a vacancy," I said, with my mouth full. "I signed up."

My mother looked at me.

My father looked at me.

My brother looked at me.

Claire sputtered, "You *what*? *My* sister?

My *sister* is going to be some dumb rah-rah?"

It was the "my" that bothered her. Other people's sisters could be dumb rah-rahs, but Claire's sister should have the decency not to humiliate her that way. I began to enjoy myself. "Just because a person is a cheerleader — " I began.

"A person?" repeated Claire. She raised her perfect eyebrows at me and set her fork down. She folded her hands under her sharp little chin and said, "What do you mean, a person? The only people dumb enough to be cheerleaders are girls. You wouldn't catch a boy doing anything that stupid. Worthless girls like Charlotte Owen become cheerleaders."

"Boys are cheerleaders, too," I said.

"Charlotte is gorgeous," my brother said.

"And stupid," my sister said. "Mother, I can't stand this. Don't let Marcy do it. You absolutely can*not* sign that permission slip."

I have heard that people can drown in an inch of water. If I shoved Claire's face into the casserole, would she drown in garlic gravy? It was nice to imagine, anyway.

"Permission slip?" my mother said.

"You have to agree that I'm in good health and that I can make all games and practices. It's the very same slip you sign for Tuck every time he joins a team," I said, subtly demonstrating that what worked for Tuck ought to work for Marcy.

"She doesn't *have* to agree," Claire snapped. "Mother, if Marcy becomes a cheerleader, it will be the most humiliating thing that ever happened to me. Anybody knows that cheerleaders are stupid empty-headed wimps. Nobody associates with cheerleaders. Cheerleading is the pits."

"I wouldn't mind associating with Charlotte Owen," said Tuck dreamily. "She's pretty. In fact, most of the cheerleaders this year are pretty. For legs, I guess I'd have to vote for Roseanne. For — "

"That's enough, Tuck," said my mother. I was sorry. I wanted to find out how Tuck ranked them all. People pay for that kind of information. However, it turned out not to be a help to my cause. My mother said to Tuck, "You mean whenever you think of cheerleading, you think exclusively of looks and not of these girls' personalities?"

"Sure," said Tuck. "I mean, that's what it is, isn't it?"

Claire smiled happily.

I said to her, "That must be why you never made the squad."

"Enough," my mother said tiredly. "I can't stand it when you bicker. Now Marcy, have you arrived at this decision exclusively because I said unkind things about cheerleaders at the game the other day?"

"Certainly not," I said, trying to look hurt. "This is what I've been reaching for all my life." My family stared at me. "The soccer team in fall, the swimming in winter, the years of jazz, ballet, and tap dancing. Even that semester of gymnastics in sixth grade was worth it. Cheerleading is the culmination of all those skills. It's perfect for me!"

"I don't believe it," Claire said into her plate. "She even *sounds* like a cheerleader. Listen to her cheering herself on here."

My mother sighed. "Cheerleading," she said, "requires no particular skill, no brains, and no real effort. It's just a cute uniform and a little dancing. It provides girls on the sidelines for people who can't follow the games."

Tuck said helpfully, "But that's a good thing for society, Mom. Who could knock girls on the sidelines?"

"Just because the skirts are short," I said furiously, "does not mean the purpose isn't serious. The purpose is to increase team spirit and spectator participation."

I was getting angry. I tried to stay calm, but both Tuck and Claire could see I was falling apart. They have perfect control over their tempers, and I don't have much over mine. I knew they were kicking each other under the table and trying to set both me and Mother off. But if I told Mother that, Tuck and Claire would look innocent and hurt and I'd be the one to get in trouble, not them. I tried to stay very calm.

Cheerleaders are always calm, I told myself.

Claire said, "My sister. A rah-rah. I cannot endure it."

"Cheerleading is a sport just like anything else!" I shrieked. "It takes effort and practice and coordination and teamwork!"

"Don't be ridiculous," said Claire. "It doesn't take anything but good legs. Bad enough you have to be empty-headed and annoying, Marcy, but you shouldn't go out on the field in a cheerleading uniform and prove it."

My father had had enough. I knew sooner or later he would. I waited for the good part. "Claire," he said, "shut up."

I thought that was a lovely line.

Claire sank back in her chair and pouted.

Tuck folded his napkin.

My mother reserved judgment.

"I also hope Marcy does not become a cheerleader. I think that's an activity for a woman who plans to spend a lifetime ironing her husband's underwear and comparison shopping for toilet tank covers. I have higher hopes for Marcy. But if she becomes a cheerleader, Claire, it happens to her, not you. It isn't your business. Got it?"

I made the mistake of smiling happily. My father glared at me as hard as he glared at Claire. My mother stirred her peas into her onions and sorted them out again.

"What is this going to cost?" she asked, rather hopefully, as if there might be a way to refuse on grounds of poverty.

"We have to supply the bloomers, saddle shoes, knee socks, leg warmers, pompons, and sweat pants," I said. "The school provides the skirt, the sweater, and the letter."

My mother brightened. A long list.

"But I still have my birthday money," I said. "I can pay for it if you and Daddy can't manage."

I thought that was a nice touch. It put my parents on the defensive — unable to pay for their little girl's heart's desire.

Tuck said, "Let me check her legs out. She's my sister, I don't usually think of her this way." He made a big deal of bending down under the table and examining my legs. I tried to kick him, but the table legs got in the way. Tuck surfaced. "Good legs," he said, nodding. "I think you should sign the permission slip, Mom. Maybe it'll give me an in with Charlotte."

"You mean on top of everything else, you're going to *date* a rah-rah?" said

Claire. She closed her eyes dramatically, shutting out the terrible events of the future. She turned to me, her eyes still closed, as if I were not worth looking at. She said, "Anybody *else* who got a letter would earn it."

"I hate you," I said furiously.

Tuck turned to my mother. "Well, look at it this way, Mom. It's better than drugs."

My mother actually laughed.

I leaped up from the table, tipping my chair over backward into the wall and knocking my water glass over. "I hate all of you!" I screamed. "You're *mean*. You don't want me to have *anything*."

I fled to my room, taking my dessert in my hand.

Nobody called me back.

I think that hurt the worst. My parents can't stand to have an argument linger. Their rule is we have to make up before bedtime. Many is the night that my sister and I, still filled with rage, kissed each other in front of our mother, closed the door beaming with sisterly love, and then finished the fight quietly, in the dark.

I stormed to my room and nobody called me back. My father didn't say, "Marcy, honey, come talk to me." My mother didn't say, "Marcy, darling, I didn't mean to snap at you. I was just thrown by all this."

And nobody said, "Claire, apologize. Tuck, shape up."

They let me go.

I went weeping into my brownie and telephoned Cath. Cath is *always* on my team.

"I wish I could have been there," she said, after I told her about the dinner table. "The sight of you Kirks locking pompons in the big final Kirk fight must have been pretty impressive."

"It wasn't impressive; it was awful. I knew they wouldn't like it, but I didn't know they'd say such nasty things to me. I didn't know I'd start to cry. I didn't know even Daddy would be disappointed in me for wanting to be a cheerleader."

Cath was very sympathetic. "Look at it this way," she advised. "You went up against a very rough team. Opposing Claire, Tuck, your mother, and father all at once? Whew!"

We were silent, contemplating the strength of character the rest of the Kirk family exhibits. I began to feel very lowly. And so unloved! Why hadn't they called me back and hugged me and made up, the way we always do?

"They hate me now," I said tonelessly. "I'm going to embarrass them publicly. Here's my sister setting trends for women, and here I am, ripping them down again."

"Forget about it," said Cath. "You have bigger problems. Tomorrow you have to start practicing. You do realize tryouts are scheduled for a week from tomorrow, don't you?"

A week from tomorrow, I thought. That's not bad. I pretty much know the words to every cheer, and I love to watch. It won't take me much effort to pick up the details of the individual cheers. Maybe one afternoon with Charlotte coaching. And a little more at home. No big deal. "Do you think David Summer ever looks at cheerleaders?" I asked Cath.

"Marcy, David Summer never looks at anything except his computer screen. Why you have a crush on a brainless wimp like that I'll never know."

"We brainless wimps are attracted to each other," I said glumly.

Cath giggled happily. "But once you're a cheerleader," she pointed out, "you'll be going on the same bus as the boys to everything. I wouldn't be surprised if this is the start of something wonderful."

The best thing about best friends is they're always willing to talk a little while longer. We have a very, very long cord on our phone, so while I talked, I tugged off all my clothes, left them on the floor, and slid under the covers. It felt really cozy there, snuggled against the sheets and blankets and pillows, listening to Cath tell me how wonderful my life would be once I became a cheerleader.

My mother knocked and walked in. Oh, good! I thought. She's going to make up. She'll sit on the bed and run her fingers through my hair and scratch my back. I said good-bye to Cath and smiled at my mother, waiting.

She was frowning at my pile of clothing on the floor, but she said nothing about it. "What's the cheerleading coach's name?" She didn't walk past the clothing. She just stood there.

Nobody in this family likes me, I thought miserably. And I have to share a bedroom with Claire forever, even when she says I'm an empty-headed rah-rah. I bet she's not brave enough to say that to Charlotte Owen's face. I bet really she's *jealous* of Charlotte Owen.

I wondered if maybe Tuck really did have a crush on Charlotte.

If so, I would ruin it. I would tell Charlotte what Tuck really thought of cheerleaders in general and Charlotte herself in particular.

"Dodie Santora is the coach," I said at last.

"Dodie?" groaned my mother. "I might

have guessed she'd have a name like that. I can just imagine the pompons waving in 1958."

I didn't say anything. I just looked at her, with as much rage as I could direct through my eyes. It didn't accomplish a thing. She was back out the door, going to her own phone in her own room, muttering, "Dodie. Dodie. What a name."

Claire walked into the bedroom. She has the end by the door, and I have the end by the window. The only separation between us is a bookcase with the shelves facing her and the back, which is covered with cork and my posters, facing me. I covered my face with my blankets and waited for her to turn the light out.

I thought, the absolutely only thing my sister and I have in common is a radio station. We both like the same rock station to wake up to in the morning.

I lay there furious at all of them, but especially Claire, undressing slowly, singing to herself, primping in front of her own mirror. "You care as much as anybody about how you look," I said, my voice muffled by the covers. "Look at you admiring yourself when it's bedtime, and there's nobody here but me."

She said nothing.

"It's just part of your image," I said, trying not to cry. "You pretend you don't care if you look good or not, but you spend as much time as Charlotte ever does trying to look perfect." I paused. "More, probably. It's easier for Charlotte."

I liked that. It made me feel better.

"Want to hear a joke?" said Claire in a dangerous voice. She got into bed and flicked the switch by her wall.

"No."

"Why are they putting artificial turf on the high school football field, Marcy?" she said sweetly.

"Don't tell me."

"So the cheerleaders won't graze after the game."

Chapter 6

The bulletin board is always jammed with announcements tacked up by anybody with anything to say. Sign up for National Guard. Pay five hundred dollars to learn speed reading. Go to Baked Potato College. Buy your maroon and white Weston T-shirts now.

When I started high school, I always thought the bulletin board would be exciting. So far, it's let me down.

Cheerleading tryouts.

It was a letdown, too. Mrs. Santora is very thrifty. She'd turned a used sheet of paper upside down and scribbled her announcement on the reverse rather than use a whole new sheet of paper. Some people (like my mother the mayor) admire thrift, but I personally hate it. I like expenditure. When I buy stockings, say, I want the ones that cost three weeks' allowance, not the scrungy, poverty-stricken ones at the grocery checkout. And for cheerleading try-outs I wanted to see a beautifully lettered, maroon-and-white-bordered scroll.

Cath shook her head. "You're nuts, Marcy. They're not going to take nuts on the squad. They'll screen you out. Remember not to offer opinions on anything during tryouts."

Kids rushed past to their next class. The sign-up sheet rustled in the wind.

"Sign it," said Cath impatiently. "Hurry. We're going to be late for our next class, Flame Brain."

"But I don't want to be first," I objected.

Cath was irritated. "Why not? They try out alphabetically, not in the order of signing. Kirk is never going to be first alphabetically."

I walked away. I didn't want to be first. Let Claire Kirk be first on all her lists. Let Tuck be first on his. I wanted my name to lie quietly in the middle of the crowd.

Cath caught up to me. "You're going overboard," she said. "Anyway, you just were first. The very first Kirk in history with detention. And Hawk has a crush on you. You're the first Kirk for that, too."

"Why don't the wonderful ones ever have crushes on me?" I said mournfully.

I was walking slowly enough to keep the sign-up sheet in the corner of my vision. Munson. Tubby, uncoordinated, plain, ordinary Munson signed up first for cheer-leading tryouts. Cath and I exchanged looks and then covered our feelings.

I wanted to cry. How did Munson see her-self? Did she think she was a Charlotte, on whom fans could gaze for hours? Munson was a great person, and I adored her, but she wasn't —

My mind caught on my mother's warn-ing.

Pretty.

She wasn't pretty, and she didn't have a decent figure. My heart sank. My mother was right. Cheerleading *was* partly girls on the sidelines. And Munson couldn't cut it.

Could I cut it? No boy had ever asked me out. There was no proof that I had any-thing to offer. Perhaps we were all kidding ourselves, standing before our mirrors, pirouetting on our lawns, practicing in our bedrooms.

Munson was pitiful.

Were we all pitiful?

She raced up to join us. I didn't want to talk to her. I didn't want to bubble about her chances and my chances and how much fun it would all be.

"Hi, Munson!" cried Cath. "You're try-ing out, too? You're brave to put your name first. Marcy was chicken. She's signing up after she's seen who the competition is."

Munson laughed slightly. "Competition," she repeated. "No, guys, I'm not competition. Especially not for you, Marcy."

We walked on down the halls. Almost everybody else was in class by now, and you could feel the passing bell about to ring. I caught Munson's arm. "But what are you trying out for?" I demanded. "I mean, if you don't think you're competition. . . ."

She'll look like a loser, I was thinking, and I hurt for her, and then I hurt for me, because maybe I would do the same. Perhaps that would be my first for the Kirks: first to be a loser.

Munson shrugged. "Fun to pretend sometimes," she mumbled, her cheeks hot, her eyes averted from ours. She walked into English class faster than we did.

Cath breathed, "I could cry."

"Me, too."

"I *know* I'm not cheerleading material," said Cath. "I'm so skinny, my hair is nothing, my features are nothing. I compare myself to Charlotte Owen, and you can't even see me on the chart. But then I don't want to be a cheerleader, so I can shrug. Poor Munson can't shrug."

"I like your hair," I said quickly.

Cath rolled her eyes.

She sat in her seat, and I sat in mine, and Munson sat between us, and the teacher droned on about great American novels.

Cath isn't shrugging, I thought. It does matter.

To be a cheerleader is to be perfect. It means you're special. You had come together perfectly: Your legs and arms and body and hair were a pleasure to look at and worth a display.

We all, Cath and Munson, too, wanted to look into a mirror and see Charlotte. Charlotte, curvaceous and slender both, her cotton sweater clinging to her perfect shape. Cheeks thin and very white, with her eyes dark circles that stared in wonder. Her barely pink lips were always slightly apart, as if you had left her breathless. Her thick, dark curly hair framed her face romantically. Even after an entire game, Charlotte continued to look sweat-free and fragile.

Charlotte was what we yearned to be.

Claire and Tuck could be cheerleaders, I thought. They're perfect. They can look in the mirror every morning and be satisfied. Nobody is kidding them, and nobody feels pity for them. And that's what they expect from life.

Perfection.

Reward.

Triumph.

Munson? I thought. What does she expect from life? She writes her name on a used sheet of paper so that she can pretend for a few minutes. All she expects from life is a chance to pretend.

When I stopped at the bulletin board again after school, there were seven names. Among them was Annette, whose mother had placed her in every class I was ever in, from swimming to computers, and who was always fractionally better than I. And Amanda and Jory, very pretty sophomores who tried out and didn't make it two springs in a row. Nancy, a new girl who'd been on Varsity at her other school. And Jinny Ives. Oh, no, please not Jinny Ives. Jinny was Charlotte's good friend, and, in fact, one of Claire's best friends — not an easy combination. When they voted on congeniality, Jinny would have to get it. Jinny had been cocaptain her sophomore year and then dropped it because of illness. Now she was hoping for one last season as a senior?

I wrote my name beneath Jinny's.

Her penmanship was sure and tall and slanting and dark.

Mine was fat and round. My pen ran out of ink so I had to go over the lines again. It was the signature of someone who never quite got it all together.

"Hurry up, Marcy." Behind me Donna and some new girl I didn't know were getting impatient. "I've gotta put my name down before I'm late for Spanish," said

Donna. She scribbled and the new girl scribbled, and now there were ten names.

I stared at the ten.

Was it an omen — my name eighth in the list?

When the results were tallied, would I also be eighth?

"Now, girls," said Charlotte. "Relax. I feel stiffness here. We cheerleaders have to be limber and easygoing and happy."

She began swaying in front of us, like a willow in the wind, and said, "Just warm up until the nerves are gone. No nervous nellies allowed."

She smiled her wonderful smile.

It seemed to me that her eyes rested longer on me, and that for me her smile was warmer and sweeter.

She led us in a long series of balletlike exercises, fluid, easy motions that led to tough, strong labor.

I think we were all slightly in love with her. She was perfect. We were a line of ten who wanted to be her. Did she know it? Could she feel it was not just a position on the squad we ached for — but to *be* her?

"You'll have four cheers to perform in tryouts," explained Charlotte when we were limbered up to her standards. We were panting on the floor. She was not breathing hard at all. "Two cheers are with a partner.

Then there are seven skills, like the split we just worked on. Don't worry about all the basketball cheers in the squad's repertoire, or about the half-time routines. The girl who is selected will learn those during regular practice."

Regular practice, I thought.

I saw myself every day with Charlotte. I thought I might cut my hair like hers, and when we stood next to each other, her black hair and my auburn hair would be perfect together.

Tuck kind of likes you, I thought. Maybe you could date my brother. I'd love that. I'd think more highly of Tuck, too.

"All right," Charlotte said. "Let's master *Weston, Best One.*" Everybody partner with the girl on her left."

The girl on my left was Jinny Ives. We were supposed to do the mirror image of each other, but I am more a follower than a leader. Whatever Jinny did I helplessly imitated, instead of going my own direction. Jinny was patient, but not because she was naturally patient like Charlotte. Because she was superior, like Claire.

"It's very hard, isn't it?" Jinny said sympathetically, since she was not finding it hard at all. "But you're only a freshman, Marcy. It's not as if you have any experience or background."

Amanda and Jory made a perfect pair.

Donna and the new girl were excellent. Annette stumbled like me. Munson never got anything at all.

I concentrated and Charlotte stood beside me doing it with me. "Oh, *excellent*," she said. "Oh, Marcy, you have it now! What a quick learner you are."

Jinny glared at Charlotte. Jinny had gotten it instantly — having been a cheerleader in this very squad for a whole year. But Jinny wanted Charlotte's approval as much as I did. I glowed in it. I wanted it all for myself, and I tried not to listen when Charlotte complimented every girl she worked with.

She worked with Munson for only a minute and moved on to Annette. It bothered me at first, because Munson needed so much help.

But then I realized that Munson was beyond help, and Charlotte did not intend to waste time. Munson would be a waste of her time.

It chilled my heart. I was grateful that I was not a waste of Charlotte's time. Bad enough I was a waste of my family's time.

"Break," Charlotte cried abruptly. "Everybody get a sip of water from the drinking fountain."

I was exhausted and walked slowly. Munson was whipped and barely walked at all. We were at the end of the thirsty line. I tried to think of something encouraging to say to her, but nothing came to me. I patted her instead. Tears filled her eyes. "Munson?" I breathed.

"Marcy," she whispered, "there's no point."

I hugged her.

I could feel her muscles fighting against the tears.

"I'm not very good, either," I said quickly.

"Oh, Marcy, you're excellent," she said. "You know you are. You look so good up there, and nobody else has red hair. You'd be a real asset to the squad." She let go of me and walked to Mrs. Santora's office, and we all knew she was withdrawing from the competition. Charlotte said, "Munson, don't go. I need you. Would you be willing to help me with paperwork and stuff? It would be so wonderful to have a girl who understands cheerleading, sort of to be an assistant manager."

I loved Charlotte for that. We all loved Charlotte for it. And Munson was happier.

The new girl who had been her partner said, "Is she *quitting*? Well, what am I supposed to do? I mean, now I don't have a partner. I think that was pretty thoughtless of her, walking out on me like this."

Munson didn't hear.

Charlotte did.

Charlotte's wide, lovely eyes grew narrower, and she studied the new girl and nodded slightly to herself, and we all knew the first judging had already occurred.

Let me be like Charlotte, I thought, and let Charlotte like me. Never let Charlotte's opinion of me fall.

Chapter 7

"Marcy, for heaven's sake! What are you doing?" my mother demanded.

"Practicing."

"Practicing what?"

"Cheers, Mother. They're very hard. I have only this weekend and Monday to get ready."

It wasn't just a matter of going down on one knee, shouting, "Fro-o-o-m-m . . . *Marcy!*" and leaping up again. It was hard to land neatly on my knee and not tip over. It was embarrassing to bellow my own name. My name sounded stupid and pretend. I wanted my name to be Susan or Valerie or even Ethel. Anything but Marcy. The more I shouted it the more ridiculous I felt.

Claire sniffed. "Cheerleading doesn't take practice," she said. "It takes the brains of a plant."

"If you're so terrific, *you* do it," I screamed across the lawn.

"Terrific people *don't* cheerlead, Marcy," she said. "That's the whole point."

It was a good thing she was inside the front hall, yelling through the screen, and I was out on the grass. The enormity of my rage against Claire was frightening. I didn't just feel angry. I felt like squashing her. With cleats.

Stop, I told myself, just stop. Relax. It's only Claire. Dumb old, successful old Claire.

But after that it was impossible to practice. My mother and Claire took turns looking out the window at me. Claire smirked. My mother sighed and shook her head, as though she had just now realized that this precious younger daughter of hers was really an armadillo, good for nothing but the zoo.

I went over to Cath's to practice instead. Cath's mother is a fine woman. She immediately said, "Marcy! My goodness! What a superb split! You are so well coordinated. I could never do that."

I did another one for her and fell over.

"That won't happen in the tryouts, Marcy," she said. "You'll be splendid in the tryouts, I can tell. May we go? I'd love to be able to see you."

Of course my parents didn't want to go.

The last thing they wanted was to witness any of this.

Cath's mother said, "Here, darling. Have some hot cider and a jelly-filled doughnut. You have to keep your strength up. I don't know where you get so much energy and determination, Marcy. Cath and I are both utterly exhausted just thinking about all the things you accomplish."

A remark that certainly whipped my family's response (you lazy slouch, you dropout, you!).

We sat in Cath's kitchen to eat.

Cath's house is sort of shapeless, like her mother. It was built years ago, but not in any really exciting period of history. You couldn't really call it anything like early American or Victorian. It's just sort of there: boxy and solid and comfortable. And Cath's mother is just like that: boxy and solid and comfortable.

The inside of the house isn't very stylish or interesting or well decorated, but I never leave without feeling warm and friendly.

Sometimes I think that people have different skills and that Cath's mother's skill is friendliness. All her possessions are friendly; all her meals are friendly; all her smiles are friendly. To know her is to feel welcome.

Whereas in my family, skills are things

you can point to. They can be described in
the newspaper, for people to consider vot-
ing for. They can be listed in college applications, for admissions officers to delight in.

Cath's mother is very huggy, like a favorite, scruffy old teddy bear.

Of course, I would never tell her that.

Who wants to be told she's old and
scruffy?

And yet whenever I think of Mrs. Mc-
Dermott, I think of being enveloped in comfortable feelings and warm welcomes.

I sat, having my cider from a chipped
mug that Claire would have made us throw
out, and I tried to sort out why people are
so different. Why does my family have to
strive? Why do the McDermotts just sit
around having cider and liking each other?
Which way is better? Or is it just a matter
of being happy where you are?

"How come I'm a Kirk?" I said out loud.
"How come I didn't come out of the Mc-
Dermotts?"

Mrs. McDermott said, "Oh, what a compliment. I'd be so proud to have you for a
daughter. Here. Have another doughnut."
She droned on comfortably about cheerleading and how my red hair would glisten
in the sun and how my long slim legs would
kick as high as the bleachers.

"Basketball season is what she's trying

out for," said Cath. "No sun. Her hair will have to glisten from the ceiling lights."

"Have we bought season tickets to the games?" Mrs. McDermott asked. "Now that Marcy is going to be on the squad we'll certainly want to be going to all the games."

My parents hadn't said that.

My parents hadn't even mentioned going to the games.

Maybe they wouldn't go. Maybe....

No. They'd have to be there anyway. To watch Tuck.

I knew my mother. She'd sit far from the cheerleading, so as to minimize the risk of having the cheerleaders block her view of the court and her fine, fine son Tuck.

The terrible anger I had felt at Claire was replaced by a terrible sadness.

My mother doesn't love me the way Mrs. McDermott does, I thought. I have to go to somebody else's house to be appreciated. But Claire and Tuck go home to be appreciated.

"Why don't you go out in the side yard and work on that spirit cheer again?" suggested Mrs. McDermott. "Let me get my coat on. It was my impression that the beat was just a tiny bit awkward there."

How nicely she phrased it — a tiny bit awkward on the beat. Not like Claire telling me only people with the brains of a houseplant would even consider it. Not like my mother making faces and twitching because she thinks it's inappropriate.

In the side yard I did the spirit cheer. Cath and Mrs. McDermott clapped and shrieked praise. I did the "Come on team, come on bold" cheer.

"Oh, Marcy, you're so excellent," said Cath admiringly. She and her mother leaned against each other to watch me. "Do Big G, Marcy. It's my favorite."

I bounced out in the yard.

"Big G, little o . . . Go, Go.
Big G, little o . . . Go, Go.
Double U, I, N . . . WIN, WIN.
Double U, I, N . . . WIN, WIN."

You have to say the Double U very quickly to keep it in rhythm, spitting out the syllables carefully to make them clear. You do this complex hand motion, swirling your pom-pon left, then right, then swooping over your head. And then this thumping kick series for the final Win, Win. When you have two rows of six girls each doing this, each row the mirror image of the other, it's a very impressive cheer.

But when your left hand goes one way and your right hand goes the other, and your right ankle hooks onto your left shoe instead of neatly curling around — what you have is Marcy in the grass like a tripped rabbit.

"Oh, Cath!" I cried, wiping uselessly at the grass stain on my pants. "I just can't get it right! Charlotte will think I'm a jerk."

Mrs. McDermott yanked me to my feet. "How many are trying out?" she asked.

"Nine."

"For how many spaces?"

"One."

Mrs. McDermott looked very taken aback. She looked at me again, and this time her gray eyes were more careful and saw more and comforted less. Her lips looked thin. She pushed her graying hair back behind her ears. "Now, Marcy, first do the hands alone while we clap the rhythm for you."

She's worried, I thought. And if Mrs. McDermott is worried, things are pretty bad. What if I don't make it? What will it be like, living with Claire and Tuck and my parents? They say any fool can be a cheerleader. So if I fail even at cheerleading, they'll know I'm nothing but a jerk and a lint-brain.

"Well, darling," said Mrs. McDermott heartily. "I think we're getting tired. Let's break for supper now, shall we?"

I felt cold. When Mrs. McD. runs interference, things are dark indeed.

Chapter 8

Tuck loves breakfast.

Every morning he leaps out of bed, takes a shower, and charges downstairs to fix himself an enormous helping of anything edible. The rest of us stand bleary-eyed around the counter trying not to miss the glass when we pour the orange juice. Tuck is frying eggs, hacking grapefruits in half, and singing the third verse of hit songs.

I had to eat. Charlotte had told us firmly to have a good breakfast. "What's a good breakfast?" said Amanda, who had never eaten one.

"Cinnamon raisin toast, a single scrambled egg, a glass of orange juice, and a Hershey kiss," said Charlotte.

"A Hershey kiss?" we repeated.

"Chocolate," she said dreamily. "I love chocolate in the morning."

I gagged at the thought. I headed for the pantry and a box of Rice Krispies.

Mother was sipping coffee and attacking a list. Vigorously, and with pleasure, she drew a fat, satisfied line through something she had finished. Never a flimsy check-off for her. When she executes a job, the pencil slash cuts off its head.

I dumped Rice Krispies into a bowl and found milk in the refrigerator. My father bagged garbage and carried it out to the curb. Claire wasn't around. Ames takes her out for breakfast at least twice a week.

I didn't want Rice Krispies. They were all cold and crunchy. I wanted something warm and comforting. And I wanted somebody to make it for me, as a sign of love. Cath's mother would make her anything, any time, and Cath wasn't even under stress like me.

I got frozen French toast out of the freezer, put it in the toaster oven, and rounded up some maple syrup. Tuck interrupted his singing to eat. I took my toast out, slathered it with butter, poured on the syrup, and took a bite.

I'd been impatient. The toast was still frozen in the middle. Little frozen shards like ice melted on my tongue.

I sighed.

Nobody heard me.

Tuck picked up his grapefruit half and drank the rest of the juice out as if it were a cup. "Great stuff," he said happily. "And another great day."

I have to live with four people like that.

I said, "Tryouts are today."

Tuck tossed the grapefruit half twelve feet across the room and made the wastebasket. Then he rinsed off his plate, mug, and glass, stuck them in the dishwasher, and dashed upstairs to his room.

My mother slaughtered another chore on her list, smiled at the pencil and said, "What did you say, Marcy?"

I turned on the sink tap very high. The splash against my tilted plate muffled the terrible words that came from my mouth. I slid everything in the dishwasher, slipped past my mother, who was adding two more chores to the bottom of her list, got my books and coat, and left fifteen minutes early for the bus stop. Some mornings I wheedle Tuck until he gives me a ride with his friends, but they always make a big deal of this act of charity, and I wasn't in the mood.

It was extremely cold.

Down the road, Christmas was coming; people had wreaths out. One yard had a sleigh. Beyond the intersection, the main road was getting its town decorations, enormous silvery-gold bells that light up at night.

They didn't even remember.

It wasn't that they were still angry about cheerleading. They had forgotten. I was so unimportant in the Kirk scheme of things, they couldn't even bother to stay angry with me.

I'm a Munson, I thought. In this family, I'm a Munson.

All day my friends gave me friendly little punches. "So, good luck, Marcy!" "You can do it, Marcy!" "I'll be thinking about you, Marcy!"

Hawk yanked my hair. "So, Flame Brain. Giving up academic things to be a rah-rah, huh? Bet old Claire will love that."

Amanda, Jory, Annette, and Donna all hugged me when we passed in the halls, as if already we shared something wonderful and special: The hope of getting on the squad was enough to make a team out of us. They were excited, buoyed up, full of themselves.

Cath bounced down the halls with me. "Guess you won't need a ride home with us today, will you? Your family will come right after the tryouts to see if you made it."

I shrugged.

"Hey," said Cath. "Don't shrug with *me*, lady. I'm your best friend."

I shrugged again. "I'll take the late bus home."

Cath puffed out her cheeks and sucked them in again and licked her lips. "You mean they're still mad? They're boycotting the tryouts?"

"They didn't even remember the tryouts."

Cath's eyebrows lifted very, very high, and then sank very, very low. "This calls for drastic action. Homicide, maybe. Torture, certainly. Sabotage, perhaps."

"They'd just rise above it," I said glumly. "That family, they regard sabotage and torture as minor difficulties to triumph over."

"At least hating your family gives you something to think about," said Cath. "You won't get nervous over tryouts because you'll be busy plotting Kirk downfalls. I have to run. I'll see you in front of the gym right after school. Keep your chin up."

Mrs. Santora balanced a clipboard on her waistline. Standing in the middle of the gym corridor, her feet slightly spread, she made a little blockade of herself. As each girl approached, Mrs. Santora yelled out her name, checked her off, and whisked her into the locker room to change.

"No audience, Cath," Mrs. Santora shouted as the pair of us turned the corner. "Scoot. Come back in an hour and a half."

"But I have to watch," cried Cath, continuing straight on. "I'm standing in for Marcy's family. I'm a delegate. I'm needed."

Mrs. Santora was unmoved.

"Deeply, deeply needed," said Cath pleadingly.

"Families aren't allowed, either." Mrs. Santora gave Cath a pretend push, and Cath made a big show of stumbling, falling, and smashing her fragile bones on the floor. "Crawl on home," advised Mrs. Santora.

"Okay, okay," said Cath, crawling forward, pushing her books ahead with her nose. She moaned a little, to add drama.

Jinny Ives rounded the corner, Charlotte close behind her.

Cath appeared to be having a seizure, and we appeared to be ignoring it.

Charlotte bounded forward, all alarm and worry.

"Don't panic," said Mrs. Santora. "Cath is crawling home."

"She crawls well," said Jinny, standing above Cath in a superior, Claire sort of way. "I guess it's nice to have a skill."

Cath rolled over on the floor, stared up at Jinny with hostility, and said, "I can bark, too."

Jinny rolled her eyes at Charlotte. "Do

you really want freshmen on the Varsity Squad?" she said. "Perhaps the rules could be changed. I mean it. I think that kind of silliness has no place on the squad."

"Stay cool," Cath advised. "I'm not trying out."

Jinny can't even remember which one of us practiced with her, I thought. Oooh, she's hateful. Another Claire.

In the locker room we all changed into T-shirts and shorts, and then walked back into the hall to wait for instructions. I was so nervous I could neither stand nor sit but sort of jumped around.

"Good idea," said Amanda. "I think I'll warm up, too."

How nice. My nervousness looked intelligent.

Jinny sat casually against the wall, leaning back as if she were bored. She left one leg — one beautiful leg — extended, and tucked the other knee up under her chin. She looked like a magazine ad.

"I'm thinking about throwing up," Jory said.

"I've had some thoughts on the same subject," Annette said.

We giggled hysterically, and one by one found ourselves dropping down to sit like Jinny, pressing our backs into the cold wall as if it could protect us from failure.

A long time passed.

"I didn't know torture was part of the tryouts," said Jory, moaning. "I thought Charlotte seemed so civilized."

"This way the faint of heart drop out before it even begins," said Amanda.

Donna pulled both her feet in to retie her sneaker laces.

Immediately I worried that my sneaker laces needed to be tighter. At the exact moment I pulled my feet in, so did everybody else in line, including laid-back Jinny. We all giggled insanely.

Mrs. Santora came out of the gym.

My skin turned to goose bumps.

"Sorry, girls. One judge is late. Mrs. Phillips from Louden High. The best I can say is, she'll be here when she gets here."

Claire and Tuck like this kind of thing, I thought. They like trying out for stuff. They like taking college boards, and they like going up against champion teams, and they like interviewing for important state-wide awards.

Maybe they changed babies at the hospital, and I wasn't really a Kirk. Inside my genes were all McDermott.

At last a breathless woman came charging down the hall. She wore a padded coat, like something movers would use to protect a refrigerator. The coat was mauve, and it sagged on one side, and her hair was partly gray and partly brown, and she was puffing.

She plowed to a stop in front of us, beamed, and cried vigorously, "I'm the other judge, girls. How awful of me to be late! Hard enough to try out without having to wait for the judges to show. Now you just blame all nervousness on me and relax, and I'll just spread out my things in the gym with the other judges, and we'll be right with you."

Definitely a cheerleader. Her whole posture was of one about to leap into the air and take on the world.

If you weren't a cheerleading judge, I thought, my mother would like you so much! She loves enthusiastic people.

I grinned at her, and she grinned back and bounced into the gym.

None of the other girls watched her go. In fact, I was the only one who had looked at her at all. I guess her wide mauve coat had been angled just for me, so that I, and only I, of the nine, did not see who walked in behind the judge.

It was her son.

You knew that instantly. The same bright eyes, the same flop in his hair, the same bounce in his step.

But there was no dowdy, mauve, padded cloth coat here.

There was this great-looking jock, grinning at all of us, books on his hip, comb in his pocket. His jeans were new and stiff and looked uncomfortable, but his shirt and sweater were very old. He seemed oddly split: half shiny new, half faded old.

And, oh, wow, was he handsome!

"Hey, good luck," he said grinning.

"Who are you?" Annette asked.

"Her kid," said the boy, gesturing with his shoulder toward the gym. "I go to Louden High. Your enemy. I had to come with Mom because we got our schedules all messed up, and there wasn't time to drop me at home. Guess I'll just have to sit here with you and wait for the tryouts to be over."

If you'd come earlier, I thought, it wouldn't have been such torture waiting. You are very scenic.

The gym door whapped open, slamming brutally against the tiles. The tiles are used to it. They cracked in all the same places. Mrs. Phillips said, "Whoops. Sorry about that. Got to watch this door, huh?" We nodded meaninglessly. We cared about her son, not about the door.

Severely, Mrs. Phillips said, "Brendan."

We smiled. Now we knew his name.

"Go to the library or something." Even more severely. As if expecting rebellion. "I will see you later."

It's always fun to see how mothers and sons act together. We fixed our eyes on Brendan.

"Aw, Mom," he began.

Mom said, "Brendan. There will be no discussion." All our heads swung to watch Mom's face and see if she looked as severe as she sounded. "There will be no flirting. There will be a quick march to the library."

Nine heads swung back to Brendan. Brendan grinned at us, shrugged, and saluted his mother, heels coming together in what would have been a click if he'd been wearing hard shoes, but was just a squeaky whoof in his thick padded sneakers. "Yes, Admiral!" he said sharply. He made an about face and marched with exaggerated care to the end of the hall, made a right angle turn, yelled out, "Annd — dis-*missed*!"

He vanished.

Mrs. Phillips looked irked.

I looked back down the vacant corridor and fell in love with the boy who was no longer there.

The body, the smile, the laugh, the shrug, the march — all perfect.

Of course, I would never see him again. It wasn't going to be an easy crush to maintain. I was already forgetting his features. But it was good to know that Louden High had this kind of thing to offer. When we had games at Louden, I would be sure to look around. Charlotte called us in. I forgot Brendan.

In single file, we jogged into the gym, our hands tucked lightly on our hips. Twice we circled past the judges, trying to smile and look lighthearted. I kept yawning. It's hard to run when you're yawning. I kept putting my hand up to cover my mouth, which is definitely not correct procedure for cheerleaders. I don't think cheerleaders are allowed to yawn, anyhow. It shows a lack of spirit, or something.

They lined us up along the wall.

The judges — Mrs. Santora, Mrs. Phillips, a woman I didn't know, and Charlotte — sat at a cafeteria table with their clipboards next to them and stacks of papers. Each stack has a paper with my name on it, I thought. And categories to grade me in. Plain white columns waiting for numbers.

I turned away quickly to look at the wall. We were on the padding side, beneath the basket. The padding was thick and maroon. A few inches from my face was a big gouge. I wondered what unfortunate athlete had run into it hard enough to tear it like that.

The first test was to run up, beaming and laughing, and do this little midair kick that Mrs. Santora is fond of (possibly because

Charlotte looks like Olympic material doing it) and cry out, "Hello! And good luck! From . . . Marcy!"

My kick was fine. Unfortunately, I wasn't in midair when I did it. I was very close to the gym floor. I bent my whole foot backwards and yelped in pain. "From . . . Marcy!" I whimpered.

The judges looked at me expressionlessly.

I stood up and debated asking for a second chance, but the words didn't come out. Charlotte gestured at me to move along. I ran back to the end of the line and stared into the maroon padding.

"It was a nice try," said Jinny, in front of me.

Hers had been perfect.

The second test was to race up, shout a boy's name, and end with a split, and get up gracefully. "Way to go — *Jeff*!" I yelled, and flung myself into the air, did a perfect split, and couldn't get up. At all. I couldn't even move. I had to roll over like a puppy and crawl to my feet. Mrs. Phillips smiled at me. Charlotte looked away. Mrs. Santora was expressionless. The other judge never looked at me once. I don't know how she graded me. She never saw me.

Every ninth time it was me again.

It took forever to reach the head of the line, and yet it took only seconds. I couldn't pull myself together. I was flustered and rattled, and I stayed that way.

It was horrible.

Before I had a chance to collect myself, it was my turn again. I couldn't remember the footing, or the words, or the timing. I watched the others desperately, trying to print it on my brain, but nothing stayed. In a moment, I'd be flying through the air, screaming out a cheer in a raw, rough voice, and then staggering back to the rip in the padded wall.

Jinny would say, "Nice try, honey."

I would refrain from kicking her.

Eight of us did a terrific, or a good, or a passable job at each cheer. I never got that high. After the *Bold Team* cheer there was complete silence, and nobody looked my way. Even Amanda and Jory turned so I couldn't catch their eyes. Charlotte took a deep breath, forced herself to look at me, pasted a falsely reassuring smile on her face, and gritted her teeth while I struggled through the next cheer.

There was something inexorable about it. Like lava flowing from the volcano and catching you by the ankles. I was trapped in failure and I couldn't get out. I pretended Mrs. McDermott was there, offering me another jelly doughnut to keep my strength up. I pretended Brendan was there, in love with me, believing in me.

I was the worst one there.

I saw myself as Munson, the girl who should have known enough to quit during practice. I saw myself as a misfit.

The very last thing was a chance to repeat any one cheer we wanted a higher score on.

I did the split.

And I did my best.

I know, because Charlotte was so glad to be able to give me a compliment she clapped and cried out eagerly, "Oh, that was *wonderful*, Marcy, that was really *ex*cellent, Marcy!" as if she were my private cheerleader.

The judges frowned at Charlotte, and she slouched back in her chair and sort of shrugged helplessly, and I knew I was an object of charity.

There were five more after me, but I didn't wait to see what they did over. I went straight into the locker room, pulled my sweat pants right up over my shorts, stuffed my other things into my gym bag, and went out. I was shaking all over.

At least they didn't post numerical scores. They weren't that cruel. They would announce the name of the winner and nobody would know who came in second and who came in ninth.

Except me.

I'd know.

The halls were completely quiet. Anybody waiting would be at the opposite entrance to the gym, where the doors opened up next to the bulletin boards.

I shivered inside my jacket and turned the next corner to where my books were still stacked, pushed up against the wall where I had rested back in the old days when I was smug and sure.

Misery washed over me. Before it had been hot lava, holding my ankles in a position of failure. Now it was suffocating, thick fog, dense as London when Victoria was Queen, and I could hardly see though my unhappiness. I was walking blind.

I almost, but not quite, tripped on Brendan.

I stopped maybe an inch short of his feet, which stuck out into the hall the way our nine pairs of legs had earlier. He looked up from his homework, grinned, and said, "Hi, Red."

I loathe being called Red. My hair is not really red. It is auburn gold. "Hi, Brendan," I said, focusing on him. I struggled to be bouncy and cheerleadery, because that must be what he liked, but nothing happened.

"They threw me out of the library," he said, still surprised. "I didn't have a pass. They don't let just anybody touch your books here in Weston, you'll be glad to know. You have to prove you have a reason to be in there. Needing a desk and a light isn't enough."

"I would have given you my pass," I said. "I forged it back in October, and they still accept it."

His interest in me picked up. "You forge passes? I didn't forge passes when I was your age."

I snorted. "When you were my age," I repeated. "How old are you now? Thirty?"

He grinned even wider. "I'm sixteen and I think you're fourteen."

"On the nose." I bent down and picked up my books.

I realized I had a lot of homework. How could teachers be so insensitive? Didn't they know I had to spend the whole night weeping in private? I couldn't be fretting about English and math and Spanish and history when I had failed to get cheerleading.

I slung my books in front of me, heaved a great sigh, and trudged off.

Brendan said mildly, "Sounds like you had fun in tryouts."

"Oh, dynamite." I kept walking. I didn't have the spirit for banter, and Brendan, with his cheerleading background and mother, presumably thrived on bubbliness.

Brendan jumped up off the floor and came after me. "That bad, huh?" he said sympathetically.

I nodded. To my horror, my eyes blurred with tears, and I was back in the London fog again. I had to turn my head away quickly before he saw. I thought of telling Claire and Tuck who had never tasted of failure.

Failure really does have a taste, too. Metallic and sick like something rancid.

"I bet you were great," said Brendan. "You certainly have the looks to be a cheerleader. So you made some little mistake. Don't let it get you down. They take nervousness into consideration and also my mother's being late."

"Yeah, but they don't take incompetence into consideration," I told him. I thought I would break down right then, but saying it out loud made it easier. The tears were absorbed into some inner part of my head, and I even managed to laugh.

Brendan patted my shoulder. "That's it, cheer up."

"I suppose your household is cheery all the time. Full of spirit and rah-rah stuff." It came to me that *everybody* in the Kirk family *except* me was a rah-rah. They were always cheering each other on, leaping up and down on each other's sidelines. I was the only one who *wasn't* a rah-rah.

Brendan laughed. "It sure is. It can get to a person sometimes, but I think it's easier to live with someone determined to be happy than somebody determined to be unhappy."

I didn't know anybody determined to be unhappy, so I had no remark to make to this. His hand stayed on my shoulder. I looked at it and thought, no boy has ever touched me before, really.

My heart turned over. I forgot the squad and Claire and Tuck and failure and success. I thought only of Brendan, and Brendan said, "So, good luck, Red."

And walked back down the hall.

And that was that.

Gone.

My first true love.

Footsteps pounded toward me from that direction. I whirled, thinking, Brendan? Running back to me? It hit him hard, too? He loves me? He —

"Wait up, Marcy!" screamed Amanda and Jory. "Hey! Flame Brain!"

I hoped Brendan heard them. Next time he'd call me Flame Brain, too, instead of Red.

Amanda wailed, "They didn't even post it, Marcy."

"They didn't even pretend we were competition," yelled Jory.

Brendan paused to listen. The girls didn't glance at him. You two are nut cases, I thought. Flying by Brendan like seagulls? To tell me we didn't make the slot?

"Jinny Ives got it," said Amanda, reaching me. She was crying. Tears tracked down her cheeks, and because her chin was very pointy, the two tracks turned in together and met beneath her lips. "I'm so mad! They could at least pretend the rest of us had a chance!"

Jory was shivering. "You should see Jinny. Prancing around in the locker room like she's something special."

"But she is," I said. "She's the one who made it."

"Charlotte's hugging her," said Amanda. "Measuring her for her uniform. I think it's very insensitive. Charlotte could have waited to do that until after the rest of us left."

But she was wrong.

If cheerleading really was competition, then the losers had to stand there and take the loss in front of everybody, just like in football and basketball and soccer. The worst part of losing is shaking hands with the winners. I bet none of us shook hands with Jinny, I thought. Maybe we're not really sports people.

Nobody spoke again.

We walked out together, wanting to be the special one with Charlotte and knowing we were just ordinary girls who didn't make it.

Jory and Amanda sprinted toward Jory's mother's car, waiting. "Need a ride?" Jory shouted back, as an afterthought. I shook my head no. I didn't want to listen to them complain that they had been treated unfairly. Nobody had treated me unfairly. I just hadn't been good.

The late bus was long gone.

I would have to take the city bus. I walked over the wide school lawn, faded now to tawny winter colors and rutted where boys had spun wheelies and ruined the grass on some damp autumn day. Two blocks down I waited for the bus, so cold that I hurt.

A car went by, honking. I thought it might be Ames and Claire, but I didn't recognize the vehicle. The passenger window was rolled swiftly down. Brendan stuck his head out. "Hey, Flame Brain!" he yelled, and the car moved on and vanished for good.

It was a gift.

One thing had come of that terrible afternoon.

A boy had bothered to flirt.

Of course, it was a boy I would never see again, but when you feel as rotten as I did, you grab at any crumb.

How would I tell my family?

Maybe I wouldn't even have to. Maybe they'd forgotten the tryouts entirely and wouldn't even ask. And if I did tell them?

Would there be sympathy? Of course not. They'd be relieved.

No rah-rah in the family to disgrace us all.

London fog descended on me again, wrapping me in blind, thick, damp grief.

I want to be pretty and appealing, I thought desperately, dancing in front of a crowd, part of a special group.

I want to be a winner, too.

And I'm not.

Chapter 9

It was dark when the bus stopped near my corner. The streetlights had come on. I walked from one pool of light to the next. The street was abandoned. It was too cold for neighborhood kids to be outdoors.

Ours is a street of four house styles, and every one has a kitchen window facing south. I could look into each kitchen I passed. Every family except mine grew plants in the kitchen window. Kirks have no time to water anything.

My books had never been heavier, nor my coat thinner. I dragged, shivering, down the sidewalk.

The entire house was lit up. Our family is spendthrift about electricity. Nobody had pulled the shades down, either, and it was a voyeur's delight.

Framed in the front storm door of the house was a bouquet of helium balloons. Shining pearly white and deep maroon and mylar silver. The school colors. Yay, rah-rah, Weston.

Neither Claire nor Ames was romantic. Their idea of romance was to have the tires rotated on his car before they drove to a regional meeting of Young State Leaders of the Future. So it wasn't a gift from Ames to Claire.

I was closer. I could see that two real pompons were tied to the bottom of the bouquet. Maroon and white pompons. Weston Varsity Cheerleading pompons.

Pompons are expensive. Special-ordered in your school colors, they are thick, heavy handles of plastic strips. These were used pompons, which is better. After a few years, the fronds get wrinkled, and they fluff out more, and rustle more, and make new pompons seem slick and worthless.

My brother flung open the door and stood grinning at me. Nobody ever looked more like a jock than Tuck: broad shouldered, with a loose, floppy grin to match his loose, floppy sweat shirt and pants. "Whaddaya-think?" he shouted. "It's gonna ambush you?"

He took the five front steps in one athletic bound, landed at my feet, and gave me a big brotherly hug. I don't get them often; I just assumed this was what brotherly hugs felt like. "Hey, a little family solidarity, right?" he said happily. He bounded back up again and took the two fluffy pompons off the balloon bouquet and did a mock cheer with them. "I borrowed Charlotte's pompons, and we all chipped in for the bouquet. Gotta celebrate, right? And Dad made reservations at The Pelican. You liked their scampi last month when we celebrated Claire. So put on some decent clothing, Marcy." He jumped down the steps yet again, flourished his pompons, and gave me a kiss.

Grinning, he looked like a cross between some zoo ape and Brendan.

Claire poked her head out from behind the balloons. "And you have to wear decent clothes, too, Tuck."

Claire tilted her chin up a little, as if she wanted me to know that a ventriloquist was speaking for her. "Congratulations, Marcy."

I got a twitch in my eye. It flickered in the middle.

"There you are!" exclaimed my mother happily. "We couldn't imagine what was taking so long." I had gotten in the way of her time-table.

"Yes," I said stiffly. "Here I am." The twitch continued. I set my books down.

Now I was inside I could see Claire better. She looked perfect. There is something nonhuman about a person who can always look perfect.

"We're very proud of you," said Claire suddenly. She hugged me, too. We've been so unfriendly for the last year that it was a queer feeling. Awkward, unloving — but a start.

They're proud of me, I thought, fighting off the gray fog of despair. And I don't even deserve it.

Claire swerved to confront Tuck. "But did you have to borrow Charlotte's pompons? Bad enough that my sister is now on Charlotte's squad. But why drag obligation to Charlotte into this?"

"It was such a good excuse," said Tuck, punching Claire several times in the ribs. Claire gave no evidence of being aware of this. "How often does a perfect excuse come up?" he reasoned with Claire. "Here I wanted to date Charlotte, and here I had a reason to sit around making special plans with her."

Oh.

So the pompons were not a celebration for me. They were an excuse to talk to Charlotte.

Charlotte knew. All the time I was trying out and failing, she knew what my family was planning. She knew how smug and conceited we all were — planning a victory dinner when there was no victory. No wonder she stayed in the locker room measuring

Jinny. What if she had had to face me and pretend and fake?

My father bounded in from the kitchen, gave me a swift vertebrae-crunching hug, and kissed my ear about ten times. When I was little, he used to do one kiss for every month I'd been alive. By the time I was around four, he quit, because kissing was taking so long.

I need them now, Daddy, I thought. Kiss me twelve times fourteen.

"Proud of you, darling," my father said softly.

"Right," said Tuck. "And now you'll be on the bus with me and the rest of the team and Charlotte and all. Good stuff."

Mother kissed my hair.

I spoke before she could begin her speech. "So what did you guys do here all afternoon?" I said. "Have a pep rally of your own?"

"More or less," said my mother. "We decided we were not being fair to you. If what you want is to be a cheerleader, then we have to stand by you. So we're all going out to celebrate. Claire had a date with Ames, but I made her put it off."

Claire waited for her round of applause, but I didn't give it.

"Tuck has a big chem lab project to do, but he will have to get up early to finish it," my mother went on. "And I" — she looked at me firmly, so I'd know how important this was — "I gave my excuses to the Zoning Board of Appeals, and I am not going to attend tonight's hearing after all."

"I'm honored," I said, fighting sarcasm and tears. My eye still twitched. It had to be visible, but nobody commented.

"Go up and change quickly, dear," said my mother. "Our reservations are in half an hour."

I went upstairs.

I didn't smash the mirror with my hair brush or anything.

It had not occurred to any of them that I might not make it. I was a Kirk. Kirks always got what they wanted. Kirks *thrived* on competition. Of *course* Marcy made the squad. They hadn't even asked me how tryouts went. They hadn't asked anybody else, either.

How can anybody in this town endure my family? I thought. Which was worse? My own private humiliation, or the humiliation of seeing how conceited we Kirks really were?

But then, what was this after all? Nothing that counted. Only cheerleading. Any dummy could be a rah-rah girl. And because Marcy was a Kirk, she couldn't be a dummy. Therefore, we can borrow the pompons from Charlotte and decorate the door for our celebration.

The phone rang. I didn't touch it. There was nobody out there I could manage to talk to.

School tomorrow.

I had to face everybody. They'd all know I'd failed, but then failure would have company this time. Annette and Amanda and Jory and Donna and the rest. Charlotte, and very possibly all the Varsity Squad, would know about the pompons, though. Would they laugh? Would they think me pitiful?

Maybe even Charlotte had believed that a Kirk never failed. Maybe she was as surprised as —

My body sagged and drooped onto my bed. Yes. I had been surprised. The most surprised of all. I hadn't thought cheerleading was that much, either. Be honest, Marcy Kirk, I told myself. You just did this to get your mother's goat. And look what it got. It got *you* failure and humiliation.

Maybe people would even tease Claire and Tuck, and they'd make life miserable for me at home. Maybe my mother had already told everybody on the Zoning Board of Appeals that I was a Varsity cheerleader, and now she'd have to admit her daughter was a failure.

"Phone's for you, Marcy," Claire screamed up the stairs. "Don't take too long. We're all ready to go, and I'm starving."

Just because it was *my* party didn't mean *I* could decide when we left. "Hello?" I said drearily into the receiver. We have a really neat phone. It's got dial memory. Claire has most of the numbers for herself. I just have Cath's number and my favorite radio station — I'm always phoning them trying to win the morning's prize for the music trivia contest. I never do. Even if I know the answer, I can never get through to the radio station to tell them so.

"It's me, Cath," said a rushing affectionate voice. "Oh, Marcy, how are you feeling? I'm so sorry. I just feel rotten all over. I'm calling because Mom says for you to have supper with us. She says she wants to sit on the couch, and we'll all have a good cry together, and then she's rented a really good movie, and we'll make our own popcorn, and we'll feel better afterward. Shall we come pick you up right now?"

"Marcy!" my mother called. "Come on, dear. We're in a hurry. You can talk to Cath any time."

"She's probably just talked to Cath a few hours ago," said Claire irritably.

"Yes," I said to Cath. "Come get me. I'll be on the sidewalk."

"Okay. 'Bye."

I put the phone down very gently. I

descended the stairs slowly, trying to make an entrance, but it was impossible: Tuck was talking about his next game. "Because Billy's ankle is bad," he said unhappily. "And if we don't have Billy, I don't think we can win against Valley Tech. They're too big, those Valley guys. Without Billy, we don't have a chance."

"They have you," said Mother warmly. My mother always says things like that.

To Tuck anyway. And Claire. I said out loud, "I'm not going to The Pelican with you. I'm going to the McDermotts for supper."

For once in my life I had silenced them all. They gaped at me, too startled for speech. My father winced. "Marcy, honey," he managed. "I guess we haven't been very nice to you up to this point, but have a heart. We all want to share in your celebration." He looked at me so affectionately I nearly gave in to him. I nearly threw myself into his arms and told him the whole thing and begged for comfort. But he added one more sentence. He said, "After all, it isn't very often we have anything to celebrate about you."

Even as it came out of his mouth, he tried to catch the sentence. Claire took a sharp, deep breath. My mother and brother both mumbled desperately to cover the meaning of the sentence.

I hurt so much it was like flu, aching in every bone and joint and muscle. "I'll be better off with a family that understands, thank you." I pushed between them and got my coat.

My mother went white. "What do you mean, Marcy?" she said, wetting her lips.

"You couldn't even help me get ready, could you?" I said to her. My voice was so thin and angry it hurt my own ears. My mother backed away from it. "You couldn't be there for tryouts, could you? You couldn't realize that maybe the late bus was already gone, and I'd have to take the city bus and wait in the cold? You couldn't bother, any of the four of you, to come pick me up at school, could you? And you didn't even ask me how it went! You didn't ask if I was nervous, or if I fell, or anything!"

They had all drawn back. The four of them were lined up against the rising stairs, the banisters like little jail bars above their heads, and shadows from the living room fell on their shocked faces. We never yell at each other.

"You're just doing this because dinner out is what we do when we celebrate. You feel guilty because you've never had a Marcy dinner. Only Claire dinners. And Tuck dinners. And reelected mayor dinners."

I was afraid I would hit one of them. I

was trembling, and I really felt like hitting. It was so weird and so sick, to have us all physically afraid of each other: we, the Kirks, the perfect family.

"Well, you can have another Claire and Tuck dinner." I buttoned my coat and shoved back past them to the door. I jerked it open. Mrs. McDermott's car drew quietly up to the walk. "Celebrate without me," I said.

"Marcy, I think you're being childish," my mother began.

I put my hand on the storm door handle. My father put a hand toward me, and I slid out of his reach. "You got what you wanted," I said. "You've kept the Kirk record stainless. You didn't want a cheer-leader in the family, and you don't have one. I didn't make it. I wasn't good enough."

Chapter 10

Mrs. McDermott ladled gravy over her mashed potatoes. She was so stunned by Cath's suggestion that she couldn't seem to stop ladling. Gradually, the gravy covered the mashed potatoes and drowned the peas and began climbing over the fried chicken and oozing onto the tablecloth.

Mrs. McDermott stared down at her lake of gravy. "I think I overreacted, Howard," she said to her husband.

"Understandable," said Mr. McDermott. "I myself am having cardiac arrest."

"Are you two laughing?" demanded Cath. "Is that what you're doing? Because it isn't funny. It's very, very serious. Marcy's family is completely against her, and I don't think she should have to live with them anymore. I think she should live with us." Cath's narrow face grew narrower as she glared at her parents.

We had had such a good plan!

Cath was an only child in a house with four bedrooms. We would empty Mr. Mc-Dermott's hobbies out of the fourth bedroom and move them to the basement. I would abandon the room where I was squashed in by Claire, nothing but a bookcase to separate us, and abandon the family who said things like, "After all, it's so rare to have anything to celebrate where you're concerned, Marcy."

And Mrs. McDermott, huggy, scruffy Mrs. McD., would be my mother instead.

"Marcy, darling," said Mrs. McDermott. She carried her plate from the table, dumped the gravy-soaked food into the trash, and started over again with a new plate. "Marcy, darling, we love you dearly. You are practically our second daughter." She set the clean plate down and gave me her teddy bear hug before seating herself. "But not really. You're a Kirk, and that's where you live."

Cath jumped up, flourishing her napkin like a pompon. "Mother! Do you mean in Marcy's hour of need, you won't help? You'll just *stand by*?" A person can always count on Cath to add drama.

Mrs. McDermott said, "I don't think her hour of need has arrived, Catherine. Her parents aren't beating her. All they're doing is being a pain in the neck about cheerleading."

"And when you get right down to it," said Mr. McDermott, looking the platter over very carefully and choosing the crispiest chicken leg, "it's nothing but cheerleading."

Cath and I fixed him with our iciest stares.

"It isn't as if it's important," he added.

Cath and I both shrieked in anger.

Mildly, he said, "I'm glad you enjoy it, Marcy. Everybody should have a hobby. And I'm glad it's strenuous. Everybody should use up energy. But all it is is cheerleading. That's not enough to abandon your family over."

Cath flung herself into her chair. The chair scraped backward against the wall, but Cath caught it and flung herself forward again, some of her hair coming very close to the chicken. "I thought my family would be understanding," she said to me. "And look at this. They're as bad as your parents."

"There's nothing bad about her parents or your parents," said Mr. McDermott. "The only bad thing you can say is that we have the same attitude toward cheerleading."

"Well, not all of us," Mrs. McDermott

said. She glanced down at her wraparound corduroy skirt. These days it barely overlapped in back because she kept gaining weight. Yet she saw herself with pleasure, and she extended her hands in a curiously graceful gesture and said very softly, "I always wanted to be a cheerleader myself." Dreamily she went on, "I had high hopes for Marcy. She'd be me." Her eyes stared at a vision of herself: twenty years younger and forty pounds lighter. Herself not as me, but as Charlotte.

How spooky to glimpse inside a parent. You like to think of them as beyond all that. But I guess nobody ever is. You always carry your daydream with you, whether you're Munson or Mrs. McDermott — or me.

"Besides," said Cath's mother, coming firmly back to reality by heaping potatoes on the fresh plate, "I seem to recall this cheerleading business started as just a way to get Marcy's mother upset. Am I right?"

I had nearly forgotten. Nodding guiltily, I said, "I guess it's sort of right. And she did get upset. But I got *more* upset. It's been horrible. It didn't prove that I could get to my parents. It only proved they don't care about a single thing except more and more Kirk success."

Mrs. McDermott made little comforting remarks all through supper, but I wasn't comforted. "Now you make an effort with your family," she said to me. "You go home and be loving to them."

Cath said darkly, "How come they don't have to be loving to her? And you can't expect her to be loving to Claire."

Mrs. McDermott said, "Well, all right. Skip Claire. But be nice to your parents. They mean well. Trust me."

I tapped my chicken leg bone on the plate. "Does this mean I really can't live here?"

"Correct. In fact, since both you and Cath have a big biology test tomorrow, I'm driving you home right after dessert so you can study study study."

Ten minutes later I was home.

My family didn't expect me. I never come home from Cath's before nine o'clock, and here I was walking in the door at quarter of eight.

They were sitting at the kitchen table. Papers surrounded them. Pencils smelled of being sharpened: that cut-wood smell of first grade.

Claire was saying, "But Mother, I'm just not sure I really want to go to that college. I know the campus is beautiful, and it has tremendous prestige, but I think I want something a little more exciting than that."

Tuck was saying, "I have the college guide right here, Claire. Do you realize how high your college boards have to be to get accepted there?"

Claire waved a hand in dismissal. "Mine are high," she said. "Now about the cost of college, Mother. I don't want you to think that — " she saw me standing silently in the kitchen door. "Oh, hi, Marcy," she said in an odd voice.

They all started.

"You're early," said Claire. "We weren't expecting you. Come on in."

My promises to Mrs. McDermott to be loving evaporated instantly. "Oh, thanks, Claire. I love being invited to sit with my own family at my own kitchen table."

What had they done with the helium balloon bouquet? I sort of wanted it after all. Without Charlotte's pompons, of course. But all evidence of a cheerleading celebration had been removed. Perhaps they wouldn't even mention Marcy's little failure, and we would skip right on to Claire's next success: easily getting into the best college of the toughest league.

My chair was filled with Claire's college catalogs and application forms. Claire scooped them up and held them in her lap. At first I thought this was welcoming, but then I realized she didn't want to risk getting them wrinkled.

We sat awkwardly. Claire doodled on the table with her pencil. It's allowed. We all do it. We have a Formica-topped table which my mother uses to figure on: She balances her checkbook there, and writes telephone messages there. Every now and then we dump Ajax on it to scour it all off. Someday it will ruin the finish, I suppose, but in the meantime it's kind of fun having the only table in town meant to be scribbled on.

"Marcy, honey," my mother said, breaking the silence, "I feel so rotten."

She did, too. You could hear it in her voice. My mother is never sick. It takes up too much time, and she's tougher than any old bacteria. "You getting the flu?" I said.

"About *you*."

It was a puff on the peace pipe being offered, and I knew Mrs. McDermott had been telling me to take it, but I didn't. I guess because they were all paying attention to me, and it was so rare that I went with it. "Oh, I bet you feel rotten," I said cruelly to my mother. "A blot on the old Kirk record. She can't even be a cheerleader. How can we hold up our heads in public, huh?"

It's not fair, I thought. My parents could pay the McDermotts room and board, and I could live there and be happy. I used to really love Tuck and Claire when I was little. Now I hate them and they hate me.

"No!" cried my mother. "I feel rotten

because you're mad at us. You think we — "

I heard her clearly for the first time. *We*. *Us*. Even my mother, upset as she was, recognized that she and Daddy and Claire and Tuck were together. I was apart.

"I think you four are all one team," I said to her, the tears beginning and overflowing hot and terrible on my face. "And I'm not even on the bench with you. I think you guys have made that pretty — no, *perfectly* — clear."

All the hurts and irritations of my life rose in my throat, threatening to spill over. I wanted to scream and swear, and yet I was afraid to say another syllable. It would never stop. I would be a broken dam.

"I have a biology exam tomorrow," I said stiffly. "I have to study."

Chapter 11

Charlotte caught me in the hall late the next day. "Marcy," she said, "I'm so sorry you didn't make it. I would have loved working with you."

She gave me a sweet smile, and it warmed me so much I almost felt as if I *had* made it. I flushed. "I wish I had done better," I said, staring at my feet. Next to Charlotte's slender feet in their darling little flats, mine looked thick and stubby in padded athletic shoes.

"There was only room for one," she reminded me, "and we really did weigh it a little in favor of the older girls. After all, you have all high school ahead of you for more chances." She smiled like the angel we all thought she was. "I know you'll make it one year, Marcy."

"I'll try," I said. I wished she would keep on walking. I felt terribly conspicuous in the hall, with people splitting to go around us as if we were a rock in the water.

"Tuck was so upset," she continued, and her face became upset, to show me how Tuck had felt.

I could not let it pass. "Oh, right," I said sarcastically. "He was just upset because he had to admit a defeat in the family, that's all."

Charlotte stepped back and stared at me. Her eyebrows curved almost in half-moons, with more shape than eyebrows ever have if left to their own growing patterns. "That doesn't make Tuck sound very nice," she said dubiously.

"He isn't very nice." I felt a minor stab of guilt. Tuck was nicer than Claire. And actually, I had always thought how nice it would be if Tuck went out with Charlotte. She was a senior and he a junior. I didn't know if that would make any difference to either of them.

"But he was so excited!" said Charlotte, half arguing with my portrait of Tuck as a not-nice person. "He literally *begged* for my pompons, and I didn't have the heart to tell him that — that — " she flushed. I knew exactly how the sentence ought to end.

"That I didn't have a chance?" I finished it for her.

The flush was very vivid on her ivory cheeks. "Of course you had a chance," she said quickly. "I think you have lots of potential. If you practice, you'll have an excellent chance this spring. Every senior is graduating off the squad, and this year that's half the girls. Yes." She nodded vigorously, and her hair swung gloriously. "You have an excellent chance, Marcy."

But I didn't want a *chance*. I wanted a sure thing, like Tuck and Claire always had.

"What exactly did you mean," said Charlotte in a low voice, "about your brother not being very nice? I mean, I always thought he was very nice."

I saw Hawk Pietro coming down the far end of the hall. He started to grin, and I knew he was going to shout "Hey, Flame Brain." The moment he appeared, Charlotte would vanish. Hawk is a little low-level for her. She doesn't have friends except in high places, and Hawk wouldn't know a high place if he flew there.

I said, hurting, "My family just loves to have an underdog, that's all. They love being able to show me up all the time. Tuck, too."

"That's *awful*," said Charlotte instantly, and I was on her team forever. "That's *dreadful*. How can they *do* that? Your own *brother*? Oh, Marcy, that's really *awful*. Well, so much for *him*. Who needs people like *that?*"

"If he's that bad," said Hawk, coming up beside us and jerking on my hair, "I probably need him. Who is he? What's he do? I'll sign him up for my team."

"Excuse me," said Charlotte, vanishing just as I knew she would.

"Hey, Flame Brain?" said Hawk, grinning. "You up to no good?"

"Yes," I said, and it was true. I had gossiped and been ugly, and no good would come of it. On top of everything else, I thought, I'm no good.

The next basketball game, we were defeated soundly.

At dinner Tuck played with his food. He'd been put in the game exactly two minutes out of four quarters and had not scored. Last year, although the team was defeated more than they won, Tuck himself rarely had a bad game. He was always buoyed up by the knowledge that at least *he* was great, even if the others weren't so hot.

This year he wasn't much, either.

"Tuck, you're the calorie consumer of this family," said Claire lightly. She passed him more rolls. "You have the two-thousand cal breakfasts and the three-thousand cal suppers. What's with this pushing a single helping in circles on the plate?"

Tuck shrugged and continued pushing.

She punched him gently in the arm. "Come on, buddy. Cheer up." She smiled for him, and tried to coax him to look at her smile and imitate it. He didn't glance her way.

Again she said, "Cheer up, Tuck."

It was a perfect opening to explain my theory about the family cheerleading act. "I always thought of you as a cheerleader," I said to Claire, "and I'm right. Now you're Tuck's personal leader of cheers, Claire." My brother and sister both turned to look at me. Score one. Attention. "Go, Tuck!" I imitated her. "Eat, Tuck! Smile, Tuck!" I added a few hand gestures. "If that's not being a cheerleader, I don't know what is." I turned to include my parents in this. They were frowning at me. "I have a theory," I told everyone, "that *all* you guys are cheerleaders. *I'm* the only one who *isn't* a cheerleader."

Claire's confusion turned to contempt. "We all know you're not a cheerleader, Marcy. It was made pitifully evident at the tryouts."

"Girls," my father said, "might we please have peace?"

"But don't you think I'm right?" I said to him. "Don't you see the Kirk family as natural-born cheerleaders?"

Claire passed the squash. I passed it, too. Squash is not my idea of people food. If I should ever raise pigs, I will feed them my squash. Otherwise it will not have a place in my home.

My mother said she didn't think cheerleading should be confused with simple family support systems.

I sank back in a huff. Naturally, nobody would pay serious attention to any theory of mine. We ate silently. Tuck ate nothing.

Claire said sweetly, "Would anyone like to hear a limerick I wrote in my creative writing seminar?"

I caught her nasty little smile. I knew *I* didn't want to hear her old limerick.

But my mother, who is very proud of Claire for being one of only eight seniors chosen to be in the seminar, said, "Oh, of course we would," and set down her fork to listen.

"Always liked limericks," my father said. "Five lines. Within my own abilities, I used to think. Let's hear it."

I made a face. We couldn't talk about my theory, but we could be cheerleaders for Claire's limerick easily enough.

Claire shifted in her seat, making preparatory sounds and motions, until our eyes were glued to her. She's very good at that. She can round up attention even faster than Charlotte in uniform. When we were all hooked and waiting, Claire rested her elbows on the table, gracefully overlapped her hands, and gently rested her pretty chin on the shelf of her hands. She recited:

If your daughter has very little brain
And the thought of her future brings
    pain,
Make her a cheerleader —
The boys will stampede her —
And her cerebrum will suffer no
    strain!

The yellow squash lay virtually untouched in a china bowl on my right. Butter still lay in little half-melted pats on the mashed top, and the barest specks of pepper danced in the mounds of squishy squash. I picked up the bowl, smiled at Claire, and dumped it on her head.

Claire let out a horrified squeal and clawed at the squash rolling out of her hair and down into her face. "You creep! You juvenile, rotten, two-year-old creep!" she screamed at me. "I'm supposed to go out with Ames in ten minutes. Now I have squash in my hair. I hate you! I hate little sisters. I'm so glad I'm going to college! I can't tell you how much I yearn to be a thousand miles from you and safe in a dorm."

"Marcy, I have had it with you," said my mother, tossing Claire a tea towel. "Leave the room now. You're being horrible. I can't believe you actually threw the squash at your sister. Go to your room."

My father was holding his napkin over his face. I'd have had to pull it away to be sure, but I thought he was laughing. Tuck was definitely laughing.

"It isn't my fault," I said to my mother. "I didn't start it. She's the one who wrote that mean limerick. But you're going to let her off because you think the limerick is clever, and you think I'm dumb!"

"Go to your room," she said with a glare.

My father controlled himself. "Perhaps you should go to your room," he agreed. "Anything to calm *this* room down."

I stormed up the stairs. I had thought he was on my side. What, was I crazy? Nobody was on my side.

As an afterthought I went into Tuck's room to listen through the closet floor.

I could hear splashy noises and Claire moaning. I gathered that Mother was rinsing her hair with the spray from the kitchen sink. But they weren't talking about me. Thirty seconds later they weren't talking about me. Tuck had changed the subject that fast, and they were listening to him.

"Charlotte won't go out with me," he said. "I thought we were getting along so well. She was kind of flirting with me, and she changed seats in math so we could sit together, and she was so great about loaning me those pompons."

I couldn't imagine telling my parents and sister that myself, but I listened on.

"Charlotte was so comforting to me when Marcy didn't make it," Tuck said next. "I thought she was really crazy about me. But now she won't go out with me."

I couldn't stand it.

I raced down the stairs fast enough to fall. I didn't care that they would know I had been listening through the closet. I flew into the kitchen, slamming a door that didn't need to be slammed, and hearing the plaster crack under the crash of the handle into the wallpaper.

I screamed at Tuck, "So Charlotte was comforting to *you* when I didn't get on the squad, was she? Why should she comfort *you*, Tuck? Were *you* hurt and defeated and humiliated? No. *I* was. You and Claire are so conceited. All you care about is your status in school. You were ashamed that any sister of yours could be blown out of the water. *That*'s why you needed comfort.

Well, I *told* Charlotte what a hypocrite you are, and that's why she won't go out with you. Because now she knows what this perfect family is really like. It's full of mean, selfish people who don't care."

Chapter 12

The next week we were in our truce mode.

Everybody was terribly attentive and polite. Courtesy oozed out of every pore. It was "Marcy, did you need a ride? I'd be glad to take you." (From Claire, who was never glad to take me.) "Marcy, you want help with that algebra? I could help you." (From Tuck, who never helped me with anything.) "Marcy, would you like to have a slumber party? Why don't you have a half dozen friends over?" (From my father, who hates large gatherings of laughing girls.)

I felt even more outside the family than I had before. I felt like a task for them, a chore to be completed. Get Marcy back in shape. Then we can scratch her off the list and keep going with the interesting things.

"I think," said Cath one day as we were

watching *General Hospital*, "I think you have made your point, Marcy."

"You do?"

"Yes. Your mother is looking very frayed around the edges. Perhaps even devastated."

"It would take a tidal wave to devastate my mother."

"Or silent treatment from her daughter," said Cath. We were at a commercial. We could talk. "My mother says it's gone beyond the point of being a point to make."

I thought about that one.

"My mother says she's disappointed in you," Cath finished.

Oh, great, I thought. Now I really don't have anybody on my side. Even Mrs. Mc-Dermott thinks I'm awful. How did that happen? How did I mess up so completely?

General Hospital came back on. I pretended my tears were for the dialogue.

Cath pulled a bag of M&Ms out of her pocket and tore it open. Dumping half in her palm and half in mine, she said, "I wish they had red ones. I like red. The colors are blah without red."

I ate all my green ones first. "Actually, I'm being quite nice to my mother," I said stiffly.

"Yeah, but in that icky-sicky way like Jinny Ives. She smiles at the bleachers and you want to throw up. Miss Maple Syrup running like sticky sap out of the tree."

"*I'm* like that?"

"To your mother. Come on, Marcy, write this one off. Let's talk about something interesting. Boys. You don't still have that crush on David Summer, do you?"

"Sometimes. Do you suppose he'll ever notice me?"

"Nope. Count yourself lucky. He's a geeky computer freak. You don't *want* him to notice you. Have a crush on that Brendan. He sounded worthwhile."

"If I were a cheerleader, I'd go to the away games, and I'd see him whenever we played Louden."

"Yes, but there'd be no way actually to talk to him," Cath pointed out. "He'd be on the bleachers, top row, home side, screaming for his team, and the only time you'd face his direction would be when the squad did the *We're going to sock it to you* cheer."

"I love that cheer."

"So do I."

Immediately we were using the living room floor for a gym, doing the *sock it to you* routine. It ends with the whole squad on one bended knee, facing the opposite team's bleachers, pointing fingers like a librarian scolding. Cath and I shouted, "We're going to sock it to you!" and leaped up, stamped our right feet hard, flung our heads victoriously, and raced up the stairs.

My mother appeared in the doorway.

"Oh, hi, Mom," I said. "I'm sorry. I know we're not supposed to cheer inside. We won't do it again. Nothing fell off the shelves."

"Or at least if it did we didn't hear it break," Cath said helpfully.

We stared at each other.

I thought, My mother is going to cry. *My mother?*

She ducked her head, an odd, shy gesture for her. Then she lifted her chin and gave us a bright enthusiastic smile. "Listen," she said. "I'm changing sides. You want to be a cheerleader, Marcy, that's what you'll be. I'll help you. We'll send you to cheer-leading camp. We'll practice. We'll buy a tape Mrs. Santora has. She described it to me. It's like a jazzercise tape, except it's cheers to practice by. We'll practice every day. I'll keep a chart. We'll conquer every bit of this stuff, and next year you'll be on that squad."

Cath had squished her face between the stair banisters and was staring at my mother.

"*We'll* practice?" I repeated. "You and I, Mom?"

"I can't do the splits, if that's what you mean. But I'll — " she struggled to express herself — my mother, who is the most articulate woman in town. "I'll be your cheerleader," she said to me.

In the living room, *General Hospital* droned on.

It didn't seem half so dramatic as us on the stairs.

Cath and I looked at each other. What could be up Mother's sleeve? Did she have some ulterior motive?

"Don't look so suspicious," said my mother pleadingly. "This is real. I really mean this."

I adjusted my sweater. "Why?" I asked. "I thought you would be happier with me having lice than being a rah-rah girl."

She winced. "I've been talking to everybody," she said, in such a long, drawn-out voice that you could really picture everybody — everybody she'd ever known — getting into the subject of Marcy and cheerleading. Ugh. "And everybody says I'm wrong. They say cheerleading is fine, and fine girls love it. It's active, involved, has team spirit, takes effort. And I should be proud of you and happy that you want to do it instead of presenting one blockade after another." My mother looked at the ceiling. "David Thorpe says I'm using emotional blackmail on you."

David Thorpe ran against her for mayor, and they've become amazingly good friends.

She really values his opinion. It was very hard to imagine elderly, bearded, experienced, old Mr. Thorpe discussing the virtues of cheerleading. "So I'm happy," said my mother firmly.

"And she sounds happy, too, don't you think?" Cath said to me. "Why, anybody would think she and Mr. Thorpe were talking about cholera, or the plague."

My mother sighed, made a face, and sighed again. Cath and I could not help giggling. "Peer pressure," Cath said to my mother. "You, Mrs. Kirk, have given in to peer pressure. Aren't you ashamed? Letting other people dictate your opinions to you? Kirks don't do that, you know. Only limp, weak people like, say, cheerleaders, give in to peer pressure."

"Cath," I said, "you're ruining it. Now that she's realized what she's done, she'll go back to her original stand."

My mother shook her head and planted a light kiss on my cheek "No, honey. I'm wrong. There are times when the majority is right, and this is that time. So, we'll work, you and I. I'll work on my attitude, and you'll work on your cheers." She smiled — the old, *vote for me* smile, and you could just feel the winning campaign waiting for us both.

Cath removed her face from the railings

and lay down right on the stairs so that five risers stabbed her, from ankles to spine. Dreamily staring into the ceiling light fixture, she said, "You're in trouble now, Marcy."

"What do you mean?" my mother said, half laughing, the way she always does with Cath.

"You forgot, Marcy," Cath said, her voice floating down the stairs. "You forgot that Kirks don't do anything halfway, Marce. You forgot that when a Kirk does something, she does it *all*. You'll be sorry now, Marcy Vernon Kirk. You'll be cheerleading from dawn to dusk. You'll be cheering in the streets, you'll be cheering on the beaches, you'll be cheering from the mountain tops."

"Stop it," commanded my mother.

Cath laughed insanely and slid down the stairs, her shoes in my hair. She ended in a clump at my mother's feet. "So what's on the practice schedule for the weekend, Coach?" she said to the high heels at her face.

My mother cleared her throat. "Well, actually, we're going up to the college."

"What college?" I said.

"I got tickets to a regional cheerleading competition. Our school has never entered it, but Dodie Santora told me they exist, so

I looked into it. We're going to observe. Seventeen squads from six states and they're all winners in some preliminary contest. Tomorrow. Saturday. All day."

"You talked to Mrs. Santora?" I said, rubbing it in. "You, the mayor, had a conversation with a woman named Dodie?"

"I'm sorry, okay? I guess she can't help it that her parents called her Doris and nicknamed her Dodie. She's really very sensible in spite of it."

"Do I get to go to this competition?" Cath asked.

"Of course. We'll make a day out of it. It'll be fun." My mother sounded quite dubious that such a thing could be fun. We all three laughed. It was so nice to laugh like that. Normal, easy laughter. It had been a while. A long while.

The contest took place in an absolutely enormous gym. I had never seen a gym so big. It was more like a stadium with a roof.

And I had never seen cheerleading so staggeringly complex.

There was a squad whose colors were navy and scarlet. They were almost military in bearing, and their cheers were marchlike, precise, and strong. Half of them were boys. What strength it added! The boys could pick up, lift, swing around, and toss the girls. Theirs was a breathtaking exhibit.

One enormous suburban high school from upstate had a squad made entirely of girls who were gymnasts. They were all very short (tall girls drop out of gymnastics early) and very compact. Cath made a few jokes about ankle-biters. But could they move! Their act was full of leaps, cartwheels, back flips, and movements I could not begin to name. All of them looked life-threatening.

The most surprising squad was one where nobody did the same thing. They all yelled the same words in the same rhythm, but some leaped, some cartwheeled, some did a sort of in-place dance, some kicked high, and some did splits. It was very chaotic.

"I don't think I like that," Cath said. "There's no teamwork, it's just everybody's individual skill."

"I wonder how they'll even judge it," my mother said. "I've been pretending to be a judge. I had to make up my categories, but I figured grace and precision, matching motions, projection of voices, stuff like that. Nothing matches there."

I leaned way forward so I could see the panel of judges. Maybe I could learn something from their expressions.

Brendan's mother was one of the judges.

I forgot the cheerleaders. I forgot everything. I began searching the bleachers of spectators hoping to see Brendan.

"Look at that girl, Marcy!" cried my mother, tugging on my sleeve. "The Asian one in the center."

"Uh-huh," I said. My eyes worked across the third row. Almost everybody was female. Anyway, Brendan wouldn't come to this. He'd have a million better things to do. I told myself that his mother needed him. He had to open doors or carry notebooks or something.

"Ooooh," gasped Cath and my mother in unison. My mother put an awestruck hand on my leg. "Look at her fly through the air."

"Wow," I said, not looking. I hadn't found Brendan in the fourth or fifth row, either. If he was in the gym, he was on our side, not near his mother. But when it finally ended, and I scanned those bleachers too, there was almost certainly no handsome Brendan there.

"I have to admit, Marcy," said my mother, shepherding us to the exit, "I just had no idea it could be so demanding. I thought of it as annoying bouncing around. This stuff was major league."

We waded through the seventeen squads. They were hugging their parents, waving their ribbons if they'd won, and hiding their tears if they'd lost.

Cath said, "Well, our school isn't major league, that's for sure. We're just ordinary."

We walked out of the immense building, gasped when the chill outdoors hit us, and headed for the car. My mother stopped walking, so abruptly I thought some oncoming car was trying to mow us down.

"That's it, Marcy!" she cried, her voice filled with excitement. "You'll develop a squad that will put those seventeen we just saw in the shade! You'll be the force to pull them together! You'll let Dodie Santora understand that from now on *ordinary* just won't do."

I was on her right and Cath on her left. She hugged us both to her. "Oh, it's going to be so terrific," she said. "First, we'll — "

"Mom, no," I said. "Listen to me. Don't let's fight the way we did all year. Just listen."

She listened.

"I want to be ordinary. I don't want to set the world on fire. I just want to be a cheerleader in Weston, doing the Weston cheers in the Weston way. Okay?"

My mother sighed. We got to the car and waited while she unlocked it. The upholstery was very cold. We buckled up and rode without speaking for several miles. Cath said, "Being ordinary isn't so bad, Mrs. Kirk."

My mother laughed. "Okay. I have the point. I'll back off."

When I said I just wanted to be ordinary, it was true.

Yet when I lay in bed that night, I knew it was a lie.

Nobody wants to be ordinary.

Didn't I have dreams of being a camera-woman, on the spot around the world? That's not ordinary. Didn't I pretend to be Charlotte? That's not ordinary, either.

I want to be special, I thought. But I want to be special *my* way, not their way.

Chapter 13

It felt as if Weston lost every basketball game that season, but amazingly enough we won ten out of sixteen games and qualified for the regionals and the states.

Tall boys don't grow in Weston. Sometimes my mother says, darkly, that she thinks there's something in the water. People living in Weston don't have the genetic background to get up to six feet. Anyway, our team, crammed with five-foot-niners, carried us further than anybody, including Tuck, Charlotte, and the whole Varsity Squad, ever thought.

Basketball season lasted and lasted and lasted. Basketball parents dragged themselves into gymnasiums all over the state, judging every game by the relative comfort of the bleachers. Everybody had had hotdogs and sandwiches for supper for so long that real meals seemed a thing of the past, or the future, but never a thing of the present.

Claire was usually our scorekeeper. It's not an easy job, with the game being so fast and the demands being so great. Naturally, she did a perfect job under stress.

The night we played Louden in the regional play-offs, my father got home at five minutes after six, Mom came racing in from her office at 6:08, and of course Tuck and Claire had already gone on the team bus to Louden, because it's quite a drive and the coach likes to get there at least half an hour early.

I tossed three hotdogs into the microwave, opened up three buns, slathered them with mustard. I took out containers of cole slaw and potato salad we'd picked up yesterday at the deli and plopped servings of each on paper plates. Hotdogs take one and one quarter minutes to cook. I tossed them into their buns, handed the plates around, got forks out of the drawer, and we ate in three minutes flat.

"You realize this is not what I wanted my adult life to be," said my father to my mother. "I had in mind long, leisurely dinners with white wine and linen napkins."

"Maybe your second wife will do that kind of thing," said my mother.

"Mother!" I cried, genuinely shocked.

My parents both laughed. "He's not getting a second wife," my mother reassured me. "The only way he leaves this marriage is in a coffin."

I shuddered. "How can you two talk that way?"

"Years of practice," said my father. "Go brush your teeth, Marcy."

"Daddy," I said irritably, "I am fourteen years old. You do not need to remind me to brush my teeth."

Upstairs I cleaned my teeth, ran a brush through my hair, and admired the way the darkest red of my hair seemed gold at night, when artificial light instead of sun hit it. I don't often wear green because it seems like too much of a cliché — red hair, green clothes — but tonight I was in a green mood. Jerking off my gray knit sweater (it's Tuck's, really, with navy and scarlet pin stripes across the chest, very masculine, I adore it) and pulled on a feminine green sweater. I fixed the collar of my blouse so I had a nice, high, white rim, put on a gold necklace, and raced downstairs.

"What did you do?" said my father. "Brush each tooth separately and apply polish?"

"Just changed my clothes. I have to look nice."

We dashed to the car and drove more quickly than the mayor of the city should to the game. Of course we had to park way in the back of Louden High because all the spaces that were convenient were long gone. Then we had to jog all around the building, hopping over puddles, and when we reached the entrance we were out of breath.

My father got out his wallet and went to the card table where Louden's Athletic Committe was selling game tickets. I shook my head to let my hair fluff out and unzipped my jacket so the green of my sweater would show.

Brendan was selling the tickets.

He glanced my way, recognized me, and grinned from ear to ear. Some people really do that — their smiles so horizontal that happiness divides their faces. "Hi, there, Flame Brain. You surviving the loss okay?"

I had to think what loss he meant. Oh, cheerleading. "It isn't easy," I said.

"You'll make it next year," he told me, making change for my father. "My mom said you had lots of potential."

Naturally this stopped *my* mother dead in her tracks. It isn't every day that people say Marcy has lots of potential. I could just imagine my mother running up to Mrs. Phillips, asking for pointers on How To Train Your Own Cheerleader At Home In Your Spare Time.

"Mom, I'll catch up to you," I said quickly. "You go on in."

She ignored me. "Was your mother one of the judges?" she asked. "I'd like to meet her."

"Mom, please." I could feel the flush spreading. I didn't want to be totally red and green, like some Christmas tree. Why couldn't she leave it alone?

"Hey, don't be embarrassed," said Brendan. "I have a mother just like this. Always in high gear. The thing is, you have to be sure and run in low gear yourself, to offset it."

"Oh, no," said my mother. "A kindred spirit. Marcy, stay away from this boy. He'll be a bad influence, I can tell."

Brendan nodded. "I sure will. I drive too fast and swear all the time and beat up on my baby sister."

Brendan's mother appeared in time to hear all of this. "Brendan William Phillips!" she said fiercely.

"They never use your middle name except to chew you out, have you ever noticed that?" Brendan asked me.

"This happens to be the *mayor* of *Weston*," said Mrs. Phillips. "What are you *doing*? What does that say for *Louden*?"

"I was being funny," Brendan said. He made change for several more people, stamped their hands so they could come and go, and tore tickets off his roll.

"I was amused," I told Mrs. Phillips.

"I," she said, "was not."

My parents decided to abandon this scene, linked arms, and headed for the door. "Should you choose to join us, we'll be on the visitors' side," my father called back to me.

"Give you credit for brains, don't they?" observed Brendan.

There was an extra folding chair leaning up against the wall. I unfolded it, dragged it over, and sat down next to him. Of course the next person to want a ticket was a Weston fan, who demanded to know what I was doing at a Louden table. "Keeping an eye on him," I said quickly. "He might try to give Weston people the wrong change."

"Thanks," said Brendan. "That's in keeping with my image, isn't it?"

From the gym came a tremendous storm of foot pounding, clapping, whistling, and screaming.

"Teams are coming in," said Brendan. "You'd better hurry up."

"I've seen them before," I said.

He had a pause in ticket sales. He said, "I don't believe you have the true rah-rah spirit, Flame Brain."

I wondered. Did I, or didn't I? Since my mother had stepped in, my future as a cheerleader had become remarkably like my future as anything else: filled with practice times, charts to be checked, hours to be filled, failures to be accounted for, improvements to be noted.

"Actually, my name is Marcy."

He groaned. "I might have guessed. A true rah-rah name. Ranks right up there with Mandy and Bonnie and Muffy."

I glared at him. No real people were named Muffy. At least not in Weston. "So you have a perfect name?" I demanded.

"Mostly they call me Brick," he said modestly.

"Brick?"

"Brick."

"Why?"

"Why?"

I heaved a sigh. He could be pretty tiring, this Brendan. Brick, indeed. What a nickname. If he hadn't been grinning at me, I would have left. "Because I'm stubborn enough to be a brick wall," he explained. "They've been calling me Brick since I was three and I began winning all the arguments."

I was very impressed. I had won very few arguments in my time. "My mother always wins ours," I told him.

"You've got to get tough, Marcy. Never give in. Never be fainthearted."

"Sometimes I can exasperate them more by being fainthearted than by being tough," I said.

He laughed. I listened to the sentence I

had just spoken and was slightly sick. Was my purpose in life really just to exasperate? Was I telling the truth here? I plotted and planned in order to be a pain in the neck.

"Got to go," said Brendan, slamming the cash box shut and handing it to an adult who had been lounging nearby. "I'm helping keep score."

"Oh, you'll be with my sister Claire, then."

Brendan paused. "Perfect is your sister?" he said.

I laughed, and nodded ruefully. "Sure is."

"We started calling her Perfect right off. We keep hoping Perfect will mess up, but she never does. Now I see why you aim to exasperate. We sit there at the score table all night trying not to cooperate so Perfect will make even one teeny teeny little bitty error."

"You getting ahead quickly?" I said.

He grinned, his face splitting with friendliness. "I think we surrendered to Perfect last time. You want for your sake I should throw a monkey wrench into her scoring this time?"

Oh, how nice it would be! A regional play-off and my sister Claire would goof up. Seven hundred fifty spectators and they'd have to stop the clock to correct her. I savored the idea.

"No," I said to Brendan. "No, let her be Perfect. It's okay. I'm used to it."

He galloped off to join the scorekeepers at their separate table opposite the radio newscasters. I spotted Cath waving a pompon at me from the second to top row on the far side. The people next to her were going to rip the pompon off its stick if she didn't quit, so I sped over, squashed a few hands climbing up, and tried very hard to fall in David Summer's lap. Failing at that, I landed next to Cath. She was the only girl in a sea of boys. "I like your position," I murmured.

She nodded. "Boys to the left of us, boys to the right of us, boys behind us, and boys in front of us. Good strategy, huh?"

"I have a new crush," I said.

"Better than this Brendan?"

"No. Brendan again. There he is, keeping score with Claire."

Cath stared carefully. While the rest of the gym shrieked with excitement as Louden made two baskets and we made four points on fouls, Cath analyzed Brendan Phillips. "I think an eight out of ten," she said at last, "although I'd prefer to be closer before giving a final figure. Could be a nine. You're improving, Marcy. Nobody could give David Summer more than a three."

Louden's cheerleaders took advantage of a time-out to dart onto the court for a cheer. They were wonderful. Two of their girls are splendid gymnasts. They catapulted around, back flipping and leaping off each other's shoulders.

"I think I am going to have a crush on their number eleven," said Cath. "Isn't he special?"

I thought he was weird, but I didn't say so. He had an antelope sort of run — graceful, lifting his feet very high, but strange and four-legged in appearance. He was much taller than any of our boys, though, and I gave him points for that. They put Tuck into the game, and Cath and I gave ourselves sore throats when he stole the ball and managed a lay up for a basket.

"Brendan is flirting with Claire," said Cath.

That of course was just what I needed. I watched them. I said, "Maybe he's asking her for my phone number."

We discussed this for the rest of the quarter. You can have a very private talk when everybody else is screaming their lungs out. "You should capitalize on this cheerleading thing," Cath said. "Get your mother to pay his mother for private cheerleading lessons."

"There's no such thing as private cheerleading lessons," I objected.

"So?" Cath shrugged elaborately. "Your mother doesn't have to know that. This way you could be always running over to Brendan's house, and you could plan your lessons for when he's home. You could sort of cartwheel around the lawn and end up in his arms."

I giggled. "I like it. It has possibilities."

But it never had more than possibilities. Somebody else kept score for Louden in the second half. I saw neither Brendan nor his mother again. Claire continued to be Perfect, and Tuck got more points than he had all season. My parents were beside themselves with pleasure.

The McDermotts left in their car, and we left in ours.

"I spoke to Mrs. Phillips," my mother said unexpectedly. "But she says she can't maintain her objectivity as a judge if she helps any particular girl. I like the woman. She has integrity."

"She has a cute son, too," I said.

My mother looked at me. She nodded. It would be hard to argue about Brendan being cute. "Just remember," my mother said, "he drives too fast and swears. I'm not about to let you date *him*."

"Mother!" I shrieked. "He was *joking*."

My mother laughed. "So was I."

Chapter 14

Ten days later they posted the sign-up sheet for spring tryouts.

This time the sign-up sheet was a large rectangle of yellow oaktag. A photograph of Charlotte standing on the shoulders of two other cheerleaders, one hand arched at her hip and the other raised high in victory salute, was framed in the middle. She looked so beautiful and so dramatic in her maroon and white, with her dark hair, her laughter and delight caught perfectly. Beneath her the cheerleaders supporting her were laughing, too, instead of frowning with the effort. The photo had a symmetry and grace that made you stand in envy.

Neat lines, each numbered, layered the bottom of the oaktag. There was a new coach and she had high expectations. She had spaces for *fifty* girls to try out.

Perhaps it was the attractiveness of the

poster that drew us to sign up. Perhaps it was the illustration of Charlotte and what we could all strive for ... or daydream of. Perhaps it was simply that to be one among fifty was much less scary than to be one of a dozen.

At any rate, forty-two girls signed up.

This time my name was first.

I used a bright blue pen and wrote large, and added my phone number because it looked serious. Everybody below me put her phone number on, too, because they figured it was necessary, and the new coach said to me, "Marcy, it was so clever of you to think of that!"

Naturally, I liked the new coach now more than I had ever liked Mrs. Santora. Her name was Ms. Hamill. She was smaller than any of us, and we were dying to see her cheer, because she was only about twenty-two and probably fresh off a cheer-leading squad herself. But she didn't cheer; she just talked about cheering.

Amanda and Jory and I worked together, getting ready. We had the tape Mrs. Santora had given my mother.

Claire said helpful things like, "Forty-two? Weston has forty-two girls dumb enough to want that?"

Tuck said to her, "Watch it, Claire. I'm still trying to get Charlotte to go out with me. We gotta be pro cheerleader."

"Ugh," Claire said.

Tuck said to me, "You know, Charlotte says she'll forgive me for being rotten to you if I shape up." Tuck smiled at me nervously. "I've shaped up, haven't I, Marce? Can I at least bribe you to tell Charlotte I've shaped up even if I haven't?"

Tuck and I laughed together, slapping each other's backs. I don't think we ever had before. It was always Claire and Tuck giggling together. What will it be like next year? I thought. Claire off at college, Tuck still home? Will Tuck and I be friends? Will Claire come back to find herself on the outside for a change?

My mother stood in the yard to watch. "I think we're in good shape, Marcy," she told me that night. "I like the way our *Weston, Best One* cheer has come along."

I had to telephone Cath to quote that one to her. Cath marveled. "Everybody but Claire is on your team now. Remarkable. I didn't think you really could bring them around."

"I didn't. They just felt like it."

But it was true. Tuck was on my team — for reasons of his own, but still, my team. My father was, my mother was. It was a funny feeling.

Tryouts came terrifyingly soon.

There was one good thing about that — no time to think. My nerves had not built up, and neither had my hopes. I knew that I wouldn't go blank with terror like before when I was too rattled to function. And I also didn't have the smug certainty that deep down my family was right — any dummy could be a cheerleader.

With forty-two of us, tryouts took three days.

The first day, waiting while forty-one girls did their cheer before me, I got very impatient. It was like sitting in the dentist's office when they're running late. At first you're glad because you didn't want your cavity drilled anyway. But then you're disgusted, and you just want to get the silly thing over with. You hardly even feel pain when the drill starts whining because you're so glad something is finally happening.

Tryouts were the same.

By the time I was at the front of the line, I was impatient, not scared. Eager to show what I could do, not cringing and flinching at the idea.

I did well and I knew it. It was such a great feeling! Solid and thick and untouchable by anything bad. Whether I was one of the six chosen for Varsity or not, I knew I had done my best. Driving home — this time my mother came for me — I told her about it.

"I love that sensation," she said. "Nothing so comforting as knowing you did your best."

"But what if I still don't make it?" I waited for her little lecture. About how doing your best is just as good a feeling as actually getting what you want. But it didn't come.

"You'll be lower than low," she admitted. "There's nothing more rotten than knowing your best isn't good enough." She listed about ten things that had gone wrong for her that year — like the hospital strike — when she'd done her best and failed. I had never known my mother to fail. It was so strange to realize that all those events she talked about at dinner with such enthusiasm were failures!

"But, honey," said my mother, "I've watched you enough with Amanda and Jory to be sure. You're going to make it. You're good now."

"You really think so?"

"Yes. And I'm going to enjoy watching the squad next year."

We looked at each other.

I knew she had rehearsed that line and waited for the moment when she could say it out loud.

But what I didn't know was — did she mean it?

* * *

The second day of tryouts I was heading for the gym to change when I saw Brendan.

I had not forgotten Brendan. I thought about him a lot. But I had forgotten the possibility that he might show up, even though his mother was judging again. I stared at him, remembering him better than I'd thought: every feature, every hair.

Oh, this is what I need, I thought. Another hot crush, just when I have to concentrate on cheering.

He was holding the door for his mother. She was leaning on a cane and wincing. "Oh, Mrs. Phillips!" I said, coming over to help carry all her papers. "What's wrong?"

She made an embarrassed face. "I got up in the night and didn't bother to turn the lights on and slammed my foot into the leg of a chair. I think I broke my toes. So Brendan's driving me around."

Brendan smiled at me. "Hey, Flame Brain."

My heart did little flippy flops. Brendan took the papers from me and escorted his mother down the hall. My flippy flops died away with so little encouragement.

I tagged along anyhow. After he got his mother seated, he said to me, "So if I'm not allowed in your library, where can I sit?"

"I'll take you up to the student lounge. I'll be waiting there after tryouts until the results come in."

Our student lounge is nothing to brag about. You get the feeling that the authorities think it's morally wrong for students to lounge. In a school with fifteen hundred of us, there is a lounge that seats twenty-five. It's a dark hole in the wall located close enough for the vice-principal to keep an eye on anybody there. It has no doors and doesn't even have the vending machines for Cokes. A lounge — and they keep the Coke machine two floors and a wing away.

But that's school for you.

When Brendan and I reached it, his eyebrows lifted. I supposed Louden had some splendid place with commissioned artwork hanging on the walls and floor pillows and maid service. "Well," said Brendan. "Hmmm."

"Yes, that's about the highest praise our lounge ever gets," I agreed. "I have to run. Enjoy the year-old magazines."

Brendan grinned. Another thing I had forgotten. What a great smile he had, the way it split his face. "Good luck, Flame Brain," he said softly.

"Thank you." Nerves hit me for the first time, a shower of fear that maybe they had started without me, and walking Brendan up here to the lounge could have finished me off. I shivered.

"Hey, stay calm. You'll be great. I know you will."

I managed a smile, flew down the stairs and into the locker room, and joined the rest. There were no longer forty-two of us; five had dropped out the day before. Now we would weed out all but twelve, and from those twelve, the six Varsity would be chosen.

Ms. Hamill bounded back and forth between our line and the judges' table. Snapping a little metal clicker between her fingers, she kept us going as if we were in a relay race. The judges were almost gasping for breath, trying to keep up with papers and girls. But they didn't ask to slow it down and neither did we. It was rather exciting that way, and we were left exhilarated and breathless.

"I just realized," Amanda whispered in my ear, "why it was so awful with Mrs. Santora. So much time elapsed between each of us that panic set in every time."

Even with thirty-seven of us, try-outs the second day lasted only an hour and twenty minutes.

Cath and Munson were waiting for me at the locker room door.

"Lounge," said Munson immediately.

"We already peeked in," Cath said, "and our boy Brendan is doing his homework up there. He looks lonely."

Amanda and Jory said they would go with us to the lounge.

Phooey, I thought. I wanted Brendan to myself. Now there would be four of us, and Amanda and Jory were his age, and I was younger.

"Would you believe," Cath said, as we trooped up the stairs, "that I have never actually *sat* in the lounge? I've been at school one whole year and never had time when I was at that end of the building."

"It's designed that way," said Jory. "That's why it doesn't have to be any larger. Nobody has any time to lounge at that end of the building."

"These school boards are clever," said Amanda.

We flew into the lounge laughing. Brendan glanced up, startled, and of course Amanda and Jory fell for him as fast as I had and began flirting like mad. They had more flirting experience, and they were better at it. Cath and I flung ourselves onto an abandoned couch while Amanda and Jory sat at Brendan's feet and gazed up at him.

Munson took in the scene, rolled her eyes, and joined us on the couch. Jory said in a high voice, "So. New in school?" and smiled up into Brendan's eyes.

"*Yuck*," I said, so loudly that everybody stared at me to see what was yucky. I looked away, embarrassed, and caught sight of my hand resting on the uncomfortable slick brown upholstery and said, "What is this yucky stuff? It's like slimy leather."

"Probably the skin of some slimy little animal," Cath said.

"Ewwww," I said, and almost got up, because I could just imagine some ratlike beast dying to make this horrid couch.

"It's just naugahyde," said Munson irritably.

Cath *did* jump up, dusting herself off, and making faces. "You mean it's made of little naugas?"

"Little animals died to make this?" I asked. "But I never heard of a nauga. What is it?" It sounded Australian — half duck and half weasel.

Munson moaned. "I thought you two were intelligent."

"Occasionally," I said. I caught Brendan's eye. "We have a lot of lapses, though."

Brendan and I laughed together. He had stopped noticing Jory and Amanda at his feet. Naturally, Cath and Munson and I kept up our dialogue.

"You could sell buttons," put in Brendan. "Sell them for a dollar apiece. *Save the Naugas. Upholster with Cloth.*"

Cath, Munson, Brendan, and I split our sides laughing.

What with an hour and twenty minutes of cheering and now this crazed laughter, we were spun out.

"I've got to have a Coke," Brendan said to me, and only to me. "Where's the machine? I'll buy you one, too."

There were four other girls in the lounge. He was not talking to any of them. He was not looking at any of them. It's just because he knows me a tiny bit, I thought. That's all.

Brendan stood up slowly, arching and twisting his body as if to relieve it of cramps, yawned, and said, "So come on, Flame Brain."

I got up.

A minidate, stuck right in the middle of cheerleading tryouts.

I'll buy you one, too.

The four girls watched me. I felt the way you do in tryouts, when you're one girl from ready, when the girl ahead leaps through the cheer, and in ten seconds it'll be your turn. Can you do it? Will you fall down? Will they like you?

"Down this hall," I said idiotically, giving him directions as if we both wanted him to go alone. "Turn at the double doors and go down *that* hall. Then halfway down is a stair, you go down one flight and double back. Then — "

"Yeeech," said Brendan. "Be my guide.

Protect me from attacking naugas."

He turned his wonderful smile on me and held out his hand, as if I might need help stepping over Jory's legs. I took his hand.

We walked silently down the hall. If the girls in the lounge said a word, it didn't carry. They were probably stupified.

I was certainly stupified.

Tryouts had exhausted me. I didn't have the energy to do anything more. Not that Brendan was making any particular demands. But just walking with him demanded something of me.

School had been over for nearly three hours. Every room was locked, and on the lower floor none of the lights were on. The school had a musty, unused feeling, as if nobody had been there in years.

I glanced at Brendan, started to blush, and had to look away.

"Weird school," he commented. "A million hallways."

"They kept adding. Every few years they'd need a few more rooms, so they'd hire an architect and tack them on. There was never any big addition, just lots of little ones. Place is a real jumble."

We had reached the Coke machines. Brendan put in change, got a Coke, flipped the can top open, and handed it to me.

That's the most gallant thing a boy has ever done for me, I thought. Not only bought me the soft drink, but flipped the fliptop off for me.

I was so pleased with such a small thing that I forgot to drink any of my Coke, and we walked slowly back down the musty corridors with Brendan sipping and me dreamily holding the icy can. Just as we came through the double doors the girls poured out of the lounge. Cath waved both her arms at me. "Hurry up, Marcy! They've posted the semi-finalists!"

My heart lurched. I shuddered. Now I took a sip, choked on the carbonation, and Brendan whapped me on the back. "No fair dying now," he said. "Go down and find out if you made it."

Brendan and I raced after the others, pounding down the stairs to the hall in front of the gym.

The yellow poster with the forty-two names was gone.

The lovely photograph of Charlotte was gone.

A piece of typing paper fluttered half-way above the heads of the tallest of the thirty-seven hopefuls.

"Somebody read it out loud!" Jory screamed. "I don't care how humiliating it is. Don't make us wait!"

It silenced everyone.

Somebody short I couldn't even see pulled

the list down, tearing it at the top where the thumbtack held it to the cork.

She read poorly, stumbling on the last names.

But we understood.

My name was seventh.

Chapter 15

"Do not *worry*," said Claire. "It is simply not *significant* that your name was seventh. It does not mean the first six are the six they liked best. The important thing is to stay calm."

"You're not calm," Tuck pointed out. "Why should Marcy be?"

Claire paced back and forth. I figured she had some stressful thing of her own ahead of her and was taking it out on my stressful thing. "I'm trying to get the time sequence in my head," Claire explained.

I wanted to be the one pacing, not Claire. Why did she even have to *worry* better than I did?

"Okay," said Claire. "Now. School ends at two-thirty. Tryouts begin at three. They should be over by four, and the results should be given by four-thirty. Am I correct?"

I said I didn't know.

Claire said, "I'm correct. Therefore, we will have the news prior to dinner time. Dinner time is hours later. We won't want to celebrate hours later. So we'll go to the Cream Shoppe and have ice cream instead and then go out to dinner at a reasonable hour, right?"

Mildly my mother said, "I think it should be Marcy's choice."

Oh, wow. We had come a long way. "I think I should get on the squad before we make any choices whatsoever," I told them.

I had the list of twelve names memorized in order. They ran ceaselessly through my skull. I was afraid of the other eleven. My friends and acquaintances and I was afraid of their very names.

"Oh, I forgot," said Tuck. "Some boy called you a minute before you got home. He said he'd call later."

Some boy called? I would kill Tuck if he could not give me more details than that. *Some boy.*

"Brian, maybe?" said Tuck tentatively.

"Brendan!" I said instantly, flooded with delight.

Claire tilted her chin. "Brendan?" she said. "The timekeeper for Louden?"

I nodded.

She tilted her chin the other way, assessing me. "Brendan," she repeated thought-fully, narrowing her eyes.

"I'm not at all sure I want you to go out with him," my mother said. "Even to joke about things like that indicates — "

And the miraculous happened.

Claire, the Claire, my Claire, said out loud, "Really, mother. Marcy is very mature. Brendan is a fine person. I like him. She can go out with him." Ignoring anything else from my mother, she said to me decisively, "Go out with him, Marcy. Don't worry about Mother."

"Oh, Claire," I said, "he's probably not even asking me out. He's probably just wishing me good luck in the tryouts. You all jump to so many conclusions. It drives me crazy."

"Think positively," Claire said. "It works for me."

Yeah, and what did you get for thinking positively? I thought. Ames. Who else would want Ames?

For the first time, it crossed my mind that Claire didn't always have the best. Ames — why, Ames was an older David Summer. A three out of ten. A computer geek who happens to drive a terrific car and spends lots of money on Claire. But not interesting or exciting or handsome. Just tall.

I looked at Claire, and she seemed out of

focus for an instant. As if she could be ordinary now and then herself.

"You've *got* to make cheerleading, Marcy," Tuck said firmly. "Charlotte is almost ready to go out with me. She said she thinks she can go out Friday. If you don't make it, she'll say it's because you don't get any family support, and then she might not go out with me."

"Okay, okay. I promise to make it. And I promise to tell her I get lots of family support."

Tuck grinned happily.

My mother's face settled slightly, with fewer lines, with more contentment.

I do have family support, I thought. Where did it come from? When did this happen?

The phone rang.

Claire jumped up and got it first. She has a lovely, lilting voice on the phone, very feminine and charming. "Hello?" She widened her eyes at me, grinned like a big sister should, and handed me the phone. "Brendan," she whispered.

I held the phone as if it were a ticket to the future, and my daydreams swirled so fast and so romantically it was like reading an entire romance book in the split second it took to press the receiver to my ear.

But Brendan was just wishing me good luck.

I sighed, but not hard. It was still very nice of him. In a family of cheerleaders, he must know the importance of being a cheerleader for your friends. He was not asking me out, he was just cheering me on.

I liked picturing it.

He got home, he put his mother's papers away, he helped his mother to a chair, he leaned his mother's cane up against the wall — and made the effort to telephone me twice.

That night I lay awake dreaming. I would be as beautiful as Charlotte and lead a life of perfection.

I fell asleep far later than anybody trying out for anything should. In the morning I didn't hear the alarm and had to rush like mad to get ready. "Why didn't you wake me up?" I screamed at Claire.

"Forgot." She brushed past me. "Can I wear your navy flats?"

"No."

"Why not? You're wearing your pink sneakers."

"You weren't nice. You didn't wake me up. You can't wear my navy flats." And to think the night before I thought Claire had possibilities. Was my supporter. Hah. She just wanted to go to the Cream Shoppe at somebody else's expense.

The phone rang. Claire grabbed the extension. "For you," she told me.

"Hi, Cath," I said.

We call each other most mornings to make sure we're doing the same thing during the day. I'd have to see if she could come to the Cream Shoppe with us . . . if I made it.

Brendan said, "I knew I had a high-pitched voice, but I didn't know it was that high."

"Oh, no," I said. "Oh, hi, Brendan. I mean, I was sure it was Cath."

"Nope. It's me. I called to wish you good luck this afternoon."

"But you wished me good luck last night."

"I know, but that one's stale now. This is a new, fresh good luck."

I missed breakfast to talk to Brendan.

I almost missed the bus, too.

But who needs breakfast? A person gets a lot more from a friendly voice than a piece of toast anyway.

A few minutes before three I went into the gym to change.

Both my mother and father were there. My brother and sister and Ames were there, with Tuck hovering near Charlotte, who was not a judge this time, since her squad was officially out of existence.

In another two hours there would be a new squad.

If I made it, I would vote for the new captain.

I shivered.

Mrs. McDermott and Cath were there. Munson was there. Mrs. Santora was there, without responsibility, but still interested in the squad and who made it.

I pulled my mother aside. "Mom, if I don't make it, what's going to happen? I mean, everybody is standing here. It's going to be like the balloon bouquet. We'll have to pretend. And all I'll want to do is go home and cry."

"I won't let you go home and cry," my mother said. "We'll celebrate anyway. We'll celebrate all those hours of practice and all that desire and all that energy. We'll celebrate that you made it through hours of tryouts and lived to tell the tale. After all that you're going to need good food whether you're a Varsity cheerleader or not. So forget crying."

I started to get angry with her for not understanding, and then I thought, but maybe *I'm* the one who doesn't understand. Maybe she's right. I could give it a try, anyhow.

I slipped into the locker room with the others. We were all terrified. Amanda and Jory were staring into the mirrors, not fixing their hair, just fastened in front of the reflections.

Where was Brendan?

Didn't his mother need him today?

Could broken toes heal overnight?

Was he doing something more important?

Would he ever call me again, to keep my good luck from going stale?

My thoughts stumbled over each other, they came so fast. I hoped my feet wouldn't do the same.

Ms. Hamill summoned us in.

She warmed us up as if we were rats in a maze. Yelling, stamping her little foot, she put us through exercises and routines.

"I feel like a horse." Amanda panted. "The woman doesn't even need a whip to train us. Just her voice."

She never let us slow down.

The tryouts literally began before I realized it. I thought we were still racing in circles, each doing an exercise, and the next girl rushing up to repeat it in perfect sequence, like basketball practice routines that take players from two lines.

But Ms. Hamill was shouting out our names, and we were actually trying out.

You had to say for Ms. Hamill, she was efficient.

Her sharp voice barked out commands.

"I don't know if I like her or not," Jory whispered to me.

"I know what you mean. But I'm not

scared the way I was with Mrs. Santora."

"Because your heart is pounding so fast you don't have time to be scared," Jory said.

Then it was Jory's turn and then it was mine, and the line shifted and we moved up and went through our turns again and did the cheers that required pairs and went back to the singles.

It was over.

I was actually sorry. I felt as if I had more to do, more skills to show off, more rounds to play.

Ms. Hamill bounced in front of us. We all looked down at her. She was really tiny, like the college competition where the squad was all gymnasts. Ankle-biters, Cath called them, because they were so low to the ground.

"Results to be posted in precisely half an hour," said Ms. Hamill. "I'm sorry we don't have an eighteen-member squad. I would love to have each and every one of you. All of you did exceedingly well." She looked down our row of twelve, her eyes locking for one moment with each pair. Somehow she managed to communicate that really, the *best* in the group was the one she was looking at.

"Dismissed," she said sharply.

We blinked. Amanda said, "I'm worried this may be the Marines, not cheerleading."

Everybody laughed, and we jogged into the locker room. Ms. Hamill shut the locker room door firmly and precisely, with exactly the right amount of pressure, and marched back to the judges' table.

We sagged with relief.

Several of the girls stayed in the locker room to talk.

One girl had to go home to take care of her little brother. Jory promised to call her the instant we knew.

I went out into the hall for company.

And I certainly found it. My entire family, all the McDermotts — and Brendan.

We sat on the open stairs in the front foyer — the architect for that particular addition liked huge, swooping construction forms — and my mother kept her wrist turned so I could watch the minutes go by. There was no need to check in case the results were done early. You know that when Ms. Hamill said half an hour she meant thirty minutes even.

Brendan sat in the middle of us. He talked with Tuck some and with Claire some and with Mr. McDermott a lot. He didn't talk with me at all.

But he was there.

Twice he caught my eye and winked.

He had a nice wink.

Thirty minutes took approximately thirty hours to pass and then we stood up, dusted our bottoms off, and headed for the posting place. Everybody else was already there.

Ms. Hamill emerged from the gym promptly on schedule, took one look at the huge group of friends and classmates and families, and said, "Quiet, please."

Nobody had been talking anyway. She had a very quieting effect on people.

"I will read the list aloud," she said. "The following six girls are now members of Weston High Varsity Cheerleading
    "Jory Devon,
Squad:
    Amanda McCune,
    Donna Leoni,
    Annette Kosko,
    Crystal Owens,
    and Marcy Kirk."

Chapter 16

"Are you sure?" Brendan said.

"Yes, I'm sure," my father told him. "My treat. Everybody. You want a jumbo banana split, four scoops of ice cream, and six toppings, have it. I'll just sit here with my sherbet and be jealous."

We were at the largest table the Cream Shoppe had, and we didn't fit. Four Kirks, three McDermotts, one Brendan, one Charlotte, and one Munson.

Brendan and I were sharing a chair.

It was very uncomfortable, and I loved every second of it. I wouldn't have moved for the world. Never mind that the edge of the chair was cutting my body in half. The *rest* of my body was pressed up against Brendan.

Next to us, Charlotte and Tuck were sharing a chair, too. They looked perfectly happy. They each ordered a hot fudge sundae, and Charlotte fed Tuck hers and he fed her his.

At the next table, Amanda and Jory and *their* families and friends were celebrating.

"Varsity heaven," said my father, glancing around.

"Yep," Tuck said. "She's a rah-rah now. Made it." He smiled a proud brotherly smile at me, and a soft, crazy, loving smile at Charlotte. Charlotte smiled back at him.

Brendan started to work on his third scoop of ice cream.

My mother said, "I'm just so proud. You know, I had so many reservations about cheerleading at first. I know I had a bad attitude. I admit it. But I started to get so excited about it. And when you were in there trying out, Marcy, I was so nervous I could hardly sit down. I wanted it as much as you did."

I caught Cath's eye, even though I didn't want to, and then Mrs. McDermott's eye, and I began laughing. "I didn't want it most in the whole world, Mom. I didn't want it at all to begin with."

"It was just revenge," Cath said.

My parents stared at us.

I nodded. "You were giving me such a hard time. You couldn't stand it that I was just hanging around. So that day you said you'd rather your daughter had lice than became a cheerleader, we figured that becoming a cheerleader would be the perfect revenge."

"Oh," my mother said weakly. "I guess I'm not going to win the Mother of the Year Award again this year."

The grown-ups shouted with laughter.

My father said, "You mean you don't care if you're a cheerleader or not?"

"I care tremendously!" I said. "I really got into it myself. Oh, Daddy, the funny part was that *you* got revenge on *me*. I ended up wanting something so hard, I had to work. Just like a Kirk."

Tuck was looking very apprehensive.

I remembered in time that Charlotte's whole life was cheerleading. I tried to think of something to say that would redeem us all in her sight, but nothing came to mind. Then I realized that Charlotte was laughing her head off. "I love it," she said to me. "What a good reason! You want to know my reasons for being a cheerleader?"

We stared at her. Charlotte, who was born to be one, had ulterior motives?

"I thought I'd date all the football players," she told us. "And I never dated one. They never even looked at me. They thought cheerleading was stupid." She giggled and looked at Tuck. "Now I'm off the squad and my four years of cheerleading is history, and what happens? A football player asks me out."

*   *   *

We stayed over ice cream for an hour and drove Brendan home and went home ourselves. We were all so full we decided not to go out for dinner until another night. And from being the most exciting day imaginable, it became a perfectly ordinary Thursday, with time for perfectly ordinary thoughts . . . like, will I hear from Brendan again? Was this just because he had to drive his mother and coincidence and basic friendliness, or was it real? Did he like me? Will he bother?

My mother made lists, executing those items finished with her black pencil stab.

My sister did her math on the tabletop.

My brother studied his chemistry.

I did nothing, of course. It's what I do best. I sat there picturing my first halftime routine, wishing Brendan didn't go to Louden, wishing he could see me in the fall, after animal trainer Hamill had taught me my stuff.

I'll have my own pompons, I thought.

It was worth it all.

It was fun, actually. Fighting for something. I'm glad I didn't get on the squad the first time. Better to fail first and know whether it's worth something to you, than to get it right off and never question the effort.

The phone rang.

Claire got it, of course. "Hello?" Her eyebrows curled way up. "Just a moment, please." She put her palm over the receiver, and said "Listen up, everybody."

I thought it was Ames, telling her some special news. Or a college, accepting her. But it wasn't. She'd come up with a limerick. And not a mean one, either.

We sat there, all of us, a family, listening. Claire, laughing, posturing in front of us, gave me a look only an older sister who likes you in spite of it all could give.

When Marcy became a young rah-rah
The boys all went silly and gah-gah
A tall one named Bren
Called again and again,
And Marcy screamed loudly, "Hurrah-
 rah!"

Then she handed me the phone.

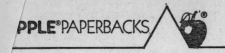

APPLE® PAPERBACKS

For Ages 11-13...

A New Kind of Apple Filled with Mystery, Adventure, Drama, and Fun!

$2.25 U.S./$2.95 CAN.

- ☐ 33024-1 **Adorable Sunday** Marlene Fanta Shyer
- ☐ 40174-2 **Welcome Home, Jellybean** Marlene Fanta Shyer
- ☐ 33822-6 **The Alfred Summer** Jan Slepian
- ☐ 40168-8 **Between Friends** Sheila Garrigue
- ☐ 32192-7 **Blaze** Robert Somerlott
- ☐ 33844-7 **Frank and Stein and Me** Kin Platt
- ☐ 33558-8 **Friends Are Like That** Patricia Hermes
- ☐ 32818-2 **A Season of Secrets** Alison Cragin Herzig and Jane Lawrence Mali
- ☐ 33797-1 **Starstruck** Marisa Gioffre
- ☐ 32198-6 **Starting with Melodie** Susan Beth Pfeffer
- ☐ 32529-9 **Truth or Dare** Susan Beth Pfeffer
- ☐ 32870-0 **The Trouble with Soap** Margery Cuyler
- ☐ 40128-9 **Two-Minute Mysteries** Donald J. Sobol
- ☐ 40129-7 **More Two-Minute Mysteries** Donald J. Sobol
- ☐ 40130-0 **Still More Two-Minute Mysteries** Donald J. Sobol
- ☐ 40054-1 **A, My Name Is Ami (For Girls Only)** Norma Fox Mazer
- ☐ 40352-4 **Our Man Weston** Gordon Korman
- ☐ 33593-6 **The Phantom Film Crew** Nancy K. Robinson

Scholastic Inc.
P.O. Box 7502, 2932 East McCarty Street, Jefferson City, MO 65102

Please send me the books I have checked above. I am enclosing $_____
(please add $1.00 to cover shipping and handling). Send check or money order—no cash or C.O.D.'s please.

Name_____

Address_____

City_____ State/Zip_____
Please allow four to six weeks for delivery. Offer good in U.S.A. only. Sorry, mail order not available to residents of Canada.

AMM861